History and Violence in Contemporary Kenyan Fiction

I0585795

This book is a collection of essays on Yvonne Owuor's writings, mainly her most acclaimed novel, *Dust* as well as *Dragonfly Sea* and her short story "Weight of Whispers". While the chapters in this book grapple with diverse themes, they generally converge on Owuor's preoccupation with different forms of violence that has dominated Kenya's postcolonial experiences, especially those around the politics of power and the roles of regional, ethnic, and gender identities in influencing such politics. Many of the chapters in this book problematize the violence of genocide, trauma, and flight as they are variously and singularly underpinned by silences that signal the failure of adequate avenues for articulation of what impact such violence has on its victims. Other chapters focus on the style of Owuor's writing, thereby highlighting the many literary innovations that Owuor crafts in order to effectively carry the weight of her concerns.

This book will be of interest to scholars and advanced students of Literature, Politics, History, and Sociology. It was originally published as a special issue of the journal *Eastern African Literary and Cultural Studies*.

Godwin Siundu is Senior Lecturer at the University of Nairobi's Department of Literature and Co-founding Editor of the journal *Eastern African Literary and Cultural Studies*. He researches mainly in literatures and cultures of South Asian diasporas and has published articles in *Research in African Literatures*, *PMLA*, *Journal of African Cultural Studies*, and *South Asian Diaspora*, among other journals and edited books.

History and Violence in Contemporary Kenyan Fiction

Standpoints on Yvonne Owuor's Writings

Edited by
Godwin Siundu

LONDON AND NEW YORK

First published 2023
by Routledge
4 Park Square, Milton Park, Abingdon, Oxon, OX14 4RN

and by Routledge
605 Third Avenue, New York, NY 10158

Routledge is an imprint of the Taylor & Francis Group, an informa business

Chapters 1–9 © 2023 Taylor & Francis

All rights reserved. No part of this book may be reprinted or reproduced or utilised in any form or by any electronic, mechanical, or other means, now known or hereafter invented, including photocopying and recording, or in any information storage or retrieval system, without permission in writing from the publishers.

Trademark notice: Product or corporate names may be trademarks or registered trademarks and are used only for identification and explanation without intent to infringe.

British Library Cataloguing-in-Publication Data
A catalogue record for this book is available from the British Library

ISBN13: 978-1-032-40825-5 (hbk)
ISBN13: 978-1-032-40826-2 (pbk)
ISBN13: 978-1-003-35489-5 (ebk)

DOI: 10.4324/9781003354895

Typeset in Myriad Pro
by codeMantra

Publisher's Note
The publisher accepts responsibility for any inconsistencies that may have arisen during the conversion of this book from journal articles to book chapters, namely the inclusion of journal terminology.

Disclaimer
Every effort has been made to contact copyright holders for their permission to reprint material in this book. The publishers would be grateful to hear from any copyright holder who is not here acknowledged and will undertake to rectify any errors or omissions in future editions of this book.

Contents

Citation Information

The chapters in this book were originally published in the journal *Eastern African Literary and Cultural Studies*, volume 8, issue 1–2 (2022). When citing this material, please use the original page numbering for each article, as follows:

Chapter 1
Introduction: Honouring Yvonne Owuor's Right to Write
Godwin Siundu
Eastern African Literary and Cultural Studies, volume 8, issue 1–2 (2022) pp. 1–5

Chapter 2
Swahili Seafarers' Musings and Sensuous Seascapes in Yvonne Owuor's The Dragonfly Sea
Jauquelyne Kosgei
Eastern African Literary and Cultural Studies, volume 8, issue 1–2 (2022) pp. 6–19

Chapter 3
Surviving the Genocide: The Singularity of Suffering in Yvonne Owuor's "Weight of Whispers"
Edgar Fred Nabutanyi
Eastern African Literary and Cultural Studies, volume 8, issue 1–2 (2022) pp. 20–32

Chapter 4
Migrancy as Trauma: Yvonne Owuor's "Weight of Whispers"
Miriam Maranga-Musonye
Eastern African Literary and Cultural Studies, volume 8, issue 1–2 (2022) pp. 33–48

Chapter 5
Rhizomic Writing and Reading of a Nation Coming to Birth in Yvonne A. Owuor's Novel, Dust
Christopher Odhiambo Joseph
Eastern African Literary and Cultural Studies, volume 8, issue 1–2 (2022) pp. 49–59

Chapter 6
The Use of Ellipsis as a Narrative Technique in Yvonne Owuor's Dust
Jennifer Muchiri
Eastern African Literary and Cultural Studies, volume 8, issue 1–2 (2022) pp. 60–80

Chapter 7

Why and to Where does Ajany Run? Culture and Femininity in Yvonne Owuor's Dust
Esther K. Mbithi and Julia Njeri Karumba
Eastern African Literary and Cultural Studies, volume 8, issue 1–2 (2022) pp. 81–91

Chapter 8

Narrating Kenyan Silenced Histories through Fiction in Yvonne Owuor's Dust
Amos Burkeywo
Eastern African Literary and Cultural Studies, volume 8, issue 1–2 (2022) pp. 92–108

Chapter 9

Let's Talk About Craft! A Conversation with Yvonne Adhiambo Owuor
Tina Steiner
Eastern African Literary and Cultural Studies, volume 8, issue 1–2 (2022) pp. 109–112

For any permission-related enquiries please visit:
http://www.tandfonline.com/page/help/permissions

Notes on Contributors

Amos Burkeywo, University of Nairobi, Kenya.

Julia Njeri Karumba, Laikipia University, Nakuru, Kenya.

Jauquelyne Kosgei, Wits Institute for Social and Economic Research (WiSER), University of the Witwatersrand, Johannesburg, South Africa.

Miriam Maranga-Musonye, Department of Literature, University of Nairobi, Kenya.

Esther K. Mbithi, Department of Literature, Linguistics & Foreign Languages, Kenyatta University, Nairobi, Kenya.

Jennifer Muchiri, Department of Literature, University of Nairobi, Kenya.

Edgar Fred Nabutanyi, Department of Literature, Makerere University, Kampala, Uganda.

Christopher Odhiambo Joseph, Department of Literature, Linguistics, Foreign Languages and Film Studies, School of Arts and Social Sciences, Moi University, Kenya.

Godwin Siundu, Department of Literature, University of Nairobi, Kenya.

Tina Steiner, Department of English, Stellenbosch University, South Africa.

Introduction

Godwin Siundu

It has been something of a tradition in literary scholarship that authors and other cultural artists whose works spur or alter debates in literary circles are honoured by collective scholarly projects, including special issues of journals. In the wider eastern Africa of post-2000, one author who certainly deserves such an honour is Yvonne Owuor, whose novels *Dust* (2013) and *The Dragonfly Sea* (2019) enjoy wide circulation and near-global critical acclaim, going by the journal articles, book chapters, conference presentations, and even translations into different languages across the world that the works have variously attracted. Owuor's other works, although relatively limited in circulation and popularity, still make profound statements about aspects affecting different regions in and people of East Africa. For these and related reasons, we dedicate this journal issue to the works and thoughts of Yvonne Owuor.

Somewhat regrettably, our honouring the literary and cultural thoughts of Owuor comes late in the day for someone who gained continental Africa's critical attention when she won the Caine Prize for African Writing for her short story, "Weight of Whispers", back in 2003. Since then, Owuor's influence as a writer, philosopher of modern times, and public intellectual has grown tremendously. Regarding her fiction, which is the focus of all articles in this issue, Owuor is acclaimed for two main reasons. First is her dexterous blend of narrative ingenuity that pays homage to the tradition of storytelling that has been the pride of African literatures since the precolonial days. By writing in this manner, Owuor's fiction is a salute to the literariness of writing, something that makes reading her works a joyful and rewarding experience. Second, Owuor commands admiration and respect for her decision to confront and reconceptualise some of the troubling questions of modern times, notably the inbuilt exclusionary logics of national histories, boundaries, and their mediation of local and international encounters with different people. Specifically, Owuor's sensitive problematisation of systemic violence and narrative subjectivity of global histories — at least versions that implicate Kenya and East Africa — is a daring statement on the necessity of critical appraisal of the present as a gate-pass to a future of dignified and humane encounters between and among different people within the bounds of national citizenship and beyond.

Noteworthy as well is Owuor's creative and discursive versatility. Despite, or perhaps in spite of, her remarkable fame as a Kenyan novelist with a cosmopolitan orientation, she continues to actively assert her public intellectual standing via all available spaces: social media quips, newspaper and magazine interviews, public engagements in conferences, and other avenues by which contemporary creative and critical theories are forged. Through this, Owuor extends the conversations on Kenyan writings beyond the pioneering works of Ngũgĩ wa Thiong'o, Meja Mwangi, Grace Ogot, Rebecca Njau, Marjorie Oludhe Macgoye, Leonard Kibera, and a host of many other Kenyan writers who beamed light on diverse aspects of Kenya's journey of 'coming to birth', to borrow Macgoye's (1986) phrase that is also the title of her most celebrated novel.

Owuor's value to Kenya is also because she raised for greater visibility more current works emerging from her contemporaries and later generation of writers. For all these writers, the whole spectrum of post-colonial experiences and challenges offer critical writing material, and their works have attracted comparisons and contrasts with Owuor's oeuvre. Some of these writers are also award winners: Binyavanga Wainaina, founder of *Kwani?* and whose short story, "Discovering Home", won the 2002 Caine Prize for African Writing; John Sibi Okumu, who was recently honoured with the Carthage Theatre Festivals Lifetime Achievement Award; Ng'ang'a Mbugua and Kinyanjui Kombani, each of whom has won Kenya's Wahome Mutahi Literary Prize and the Jomo Kenyatta Prize for Literature. These writers may have attracted less critical attention than Owuor, arguably due to the dynamics of local publishing and its notoriously poor distribution networks and not their quality of thought or style of rendition. Nevertheless, these writers and their works provide critical impulses of thought and possible refraction of Owuor's fiction. In other words, the success of Owuor's fiction and her corresponding influence globally (if translations into other languages is a parameter) are partly because her works generally and fiction particularly pick up from local, read Kenyan, conversations among writers, extend the same, and nuance them for wider consumption and engagement.

It was for these reasons that in June 2016, the African Leadership Centre in Nairobi under Godwin Murunga and Mshai Mwangola, collaborated with the *Eastern African Literary and Cultural Studies* editorial collective of Tom Odhiambo and I, to host a two-day workshop whose theme was "Perspectives on Yvonne Owuor's Decade of Writing." The workshop attracted scholars from Kenya, Uganda, and Botswana, who held pointed conversations on the oeuvre of Owuor's creative works. From the conversations emerged a consensus that Owuor is one writer whose works acknowledge and then transcend the canonical concerns of political violence, national haemorrhage, and the near-failure of the national projects to demonstrate how these dynamics alter the lives and experiences of individuals and families in Kenya and the wider eastern Africa. It was, therefore, unsurprising that Owuor had risen head and shoulder above her contemporaries in Kenya and, consciously perhaps, assumed the role of their spokesperson to the rest of the world.

In fact, in a *New York Times* interview back in 2004, Owuor had told Taiye Selasi, the celebrated author of *Ghana Must Go*, that she, Owuor, had earned 'the right to write.' She continues to assert this right in various spaces, in all of which she illuminates local(ised) perspectives to deepen our understanding of the subject matter. One only needs to scan Owuor's bibliography to appreciate her prolificity as, if nothing else, a testament of her devotion to a conscientious creative calling that bears a critical, humanist edge. The most celebrated of Owuor's writings are "Weight of Whispers", *Dust*, and *The Dragonfly Sea*; short stories including "Dressing the Dirge" (2005), "The Knife Grinders' Tale" (2005); academic and non-fiction pieces; screenplays; writing clinics; and talks delivered in Africa and Europe. She has also granted pointed interviews with journals, one in this issue, including the most acclaimed — in my view — "A God Who Wails and Dances" (Koss, 2014) published in *Image Magazine*. With such expansive and deep oeuvre, it is clear that a mere special issue of a journal is inadequate to acknowledge or fully appreciate the totality of Owuor's works. The papers in this special issue, therefore, only mark the beginning of what should be a more focused reading of Owuor's writings in order to locate her firmly in literary circuits beyond eastern Africa, where her legacy is already secure.

The papers in this special issue focus on Owuor's long prose, novels *Dust* and *The Dragonfly Sea*, as well as the award-winning short story, "Weight of Whispers." Jauquelyne Kosgei reads *The Dragonfly Sea* to explore forms of local knowledge that derive from the 'personal, and intimate cartographies of the sea.' Kosgei argues that focusing on knowledge outside mainstream science critically shapes the social lives of the 'shore folks and seafarers' alike. On her part, Miriam Maranga-Musonye examines what she calls the crisis of migrancy as narrated in "Weight of Whispers." Maranga-Musonye holds that as a common trope in narrating post-colonial experiences, migrancy can be effectively deployed to temper the impact of 'disorienting psychological trauma.' "Weight of Whispers" is also the focus of Edgar Nabutanyi's article. Nabutanyi explores how 'horror' and the 'horrific' can inspire creativity. Notably, Nabutanyi still reads the short story as a text on the 1994 genocide in Rwanda. "Weight of Whispers", Nabutanyi argues, highlights 'the less explored aspect of post-genocide suffering.' Further, that the narrator's 'spatial and temporal registers demonstrate how dislocation and innuendoes of [the Kuresemanes] complicity in the genocide catalyses the family's inordinate suffering.' The Kuresemanes are thus driven by the aim of 'surviving the peace', in Cyprian Ekwenzi's (1976) phrase. Ultimately, Nabutanyi uses "Weight of Whispers" to explore the burdens of surviving the post-genocide Rwanda.

Amos Burkeywo studies *Dust* in terms of how fiction and national histories simultaneously counter-influence each other as texts, co-texts and contexts that inform or animate each other's valences. For Burkeywo, the problems of disciplinary subjectivities notwithstanding, fiction and histories are central planks around which national artifacts can be imagined and constructed. This way, society can then eschew what, elsewhere, Chimamanda Adichie (2009), drawing on Igbo folklore — the proverb 'Wherever something stands, something else will stand beside it' — cautions against 'the danger of a single story.' This, as Burkeywo implies, explains the multiple layers of narrative and history that one encounters in *Dust*.

The vertical and lateral variety of narrative complexity in *Dust* somewhat gives Christopher Odhiambo's paper its cue, which, like Burkeywo's, also focuses on how narrative style enables development of themes. Exploring the 'rhizomic writing and readings of a nation coming to birth', Odhiambo signals how Owuor condenses in her fiction multiple histories and their underlying narrative strands. Accordingly, these alternative narrative strands can be used to weave together an idea of a nation in spite of erratic and problematic national(ist) memories. Odhiambo further shows that, although this may not be apparent to an 'outsider' reader, *Dust* actually extends ongoing conversations in Kenya regarding the problems and challenges of emerging as an organic, holistic nation. This is by no means an easy or linear process, but rather a tortuous and multidirectional journey that is hardly visible but whose presence is somehow felt, as is the case with the metaphoric representation of Deleuze and Guattari's concept of the rhizome that Odhiambo invokes. In a sense as well, Odhiambo's article employs a necropolitical reading of Kenya's national histories as rendered in *Dust*. The use of death, and narratives of death, as the structuring devices in *Dust* enables Owuor to problematise the troublesome socialities and economies of Kenya's post-colonial politics.

Extending the stylistic reading of *Dust*, Jennifer Muchiri in her paper in this issue argues that Owuor uses ellipses in 'contesting notions of homogeneity at different levels', as well as in rapturing the novel form. Besides ellipses, Muchiri argues, related strategies such as 'silences, contradictions, asydenta, and paratactical sentences' contextualise the novel geographically and historically in Kenya of the post-2007 era, where national histories exist in incomplete yet competing strands.

On their part, Esther Mbithi and Julia Karumba explore the role of ethnic and communal cultures in shaping the identities of characters in *Dust*. Focusing on the character of Ajany, Mbithi and Karumba argue that if Ajany comes off as a quintessential feminine character, it is because her personality is formed partly by her ethnic, cultural and gender socialisations as recreated in the novel. In other words, ethnicity and normalised femininity shape the kind of identity that Ajany acquires in *Dust*.

Lastly, Tina Steiner's interview with Yvonne Owuor, entitled "Let's Talk Craft! A Conversation with Yvonne Adhiambo Owuor" raises questions about Owuor's inspiration for writing, how ideas of writing may emerge and be nurtured, discernible patterns in Owuor's writing, the fulfilment derived from the writing process, and the lessons learnt in her now fairly long writing career. From the interview, Owuor's voice may be picked up as illuminating or buttressing some of the analyses by other contributors to this special issue.

Acknowledgements

As is apparent earlier in this introduction, the idea of bringing together this special issue succeeded because of the initial workshop organised by Tom Odhiambo, Mshai Mwangola, Godwin Murunga and myself. The workshop was generously funded by the Africa Leadership Centre, then led by Murunga and Mwangola. The initial plan was that Godwin Murunga would guest-edit this special issue, but demands on his time as the current Secretary of Council for the Development of Social Science Research in Africa (CODESRIA) as well as other developments made it impossible for Dr Murunga to practically undertake this energy sapping project. The editorial collective of this journal acknowledges with gratitude Dr Murunga's devotion to this project. We are also grateful to Dr Tom Odhiambo (University of Nairobi), and Dr Mshai Mwangola (CODESRIA), for their initial involvement in the project.

References

Adichie, C. 2009. "The Danger of a Single Story." Accessed at https://www.ted.com/talks/chimamanda_ngozi_adichie_the_danger_of_a_single_story/transcript.

Ekwensi, C. 1976. *Survive the Peace*. London: Heinemann.

Macgoye, M. O. 1986. *Coming to Birth*. Nairobi: Heinemann Kenya.

Owuor, Y. 2019. *The Dragonfly Sea*. London: Alfred Knopf.

Owuor, Y. 2014. *Dust*. London. Alfred Knopf.

Owuor, Y. 2014. "A God Who Wails and Dances." In Erika Koss, *Image Magazine* 109. Accessed at https://imagejournal.org/article/a-god-who-wails-and-dances-a-conversation-with-yvonne-adhiambo-owuor/.

Owuor, Y. 2005. "Dressing the Dirge." In *Little Black Dress*, edited by S. Maguire. Edinburgh, UK: Polygon.

Owuor, Y. 2005. "The Knife Grinders' Tale." Accessed at https://iwp.uiowa.edu/sites/iwp/files/IWP2005_Adhiambo_owvor_yvonne.pdf.

Owuor, Y. 2003. "Weight of Whispers." Nairobi: Kwani? Trust.

Selasi, T. 2014. "The Unvanquished 'Dust', by Yvonne Adhiambo Owuor", *The New York Times*, February 28, 2014. Accessed at http://www.nytimes.com/2014/03/02/books/review/dust-by-yvonne-adhiambo-owuor.html.

Wainaina, B. 2005. "Discovering Home." In *Discovering Home: A Selection of Writings from the 2002 Caine Prize for African Writing*. Cape Town: Jacana Media.

Swahili Seafarers' Musings and Sensuous Seascapes in Yvonne Owuor's *The Dragonfly Sea*

Jauquelyne Kosgei

ABSTRACT

This paper provides an analysis of Yvonne Owuor's *The Dragonfly Sea* (2019) with a focus on local knowledges of the sea that shore folk and seafarers from Pate Island on the Kenyan coast possess. Attention is paid to how these indigenous knowledges create local, personal, and intimate cartographies of the sea. An examination of this unique, material and intimate seascape reveals the sophisticated forms of knowledge of place that exist outside science. An analysis of the intimate engagements that key characters in the novel have with the sea helps to illustrate the centrality of the ocean to the lives of shore folk and seafarers more generally. This paper reveals that embodied and experiential knowledges offer refreshing ways of engaging with the materiality of the sea.

Introduction: The Materiality of the Sea

This paper provides an analysis of Yvonne Owuor's novel *The Dragonfly Sea* (2019) that is largely set on Pate Island in the Lamu Archipelago on the Kenyan coast[1] with the view of highlighting embodied and experiential knowledges of the sea that Owuor embraces and thereby incorporates into the novel. The result, as the analysis to follow shows, is a cartography of the seas that is intrinsic to coastal people. An examination of this unique and intimate seascape reveals the sophisticated forms of knowledge of place that exist outside science.

In her Master thesis, which provides an excerpt of the novel, Owuor explains that her project in *The Dragonfly Sea* 'arises because scholarly and official narratives of the Indian Ocean have only rarely considered the Swahili ocean imaginary, particularly as a local way of knowing and mapping the ocean rooted in those with the most intimate proximity to it' (*Owuor 2014*, 93). To bring to the fore these local knowledges of the sea, Owuor attempts to capture, imagine, and represent the embodied and experienced knowledges of the Swahili Seas which, she contends, are largely unvoiced (*Owuor 2014*, 95; Owuor 2018, 164). She gained this intimate knowledge of the seas through fieldwork that she carried out on the Swahili coast, particularly in the Lamu and Zanzibar Archipelagos, during which time she interacted with shore folk and seafarers. More specifically, she interviewed Haji Gora Haji, a sailor, fisherman and renowned poet from Tumbatu island, from whose musings she forges her characters. In particular, the character of Muhidin, the leading seafarer in the novel, is based on the life of Haji Gora, as Owuor acknowledges in the text, '*Shukraan* to the exquisite old man of the sea, seafarer, minstrel, poet, living library, and world treasure, Mzee Haji Gora Haji, who is the sonorous voice for the Swahili Seas, and from whom the character of Muhidin materialized' (*Owuor 2019*, 485). Also, the character of Ayaana, the novel's protagonist, is partly informed by conversations that Owuor had with Haji Gora (*Owuor 2014*, 93). Ayaana's character is also inspired by the life of Mwamaka Sharifu, one of six Lamu islanders who in 2002 were confirmed to be Chinese descendants, a short history of which I provide below.

In 2002, experts from Kenya and China visited Lamu island to verify claims to Chinese ancestry that some of the islanders had made. The foundation of these claims lies in a 600-year-old history that Owuor brings to life in the novel, that of the connection between Kenya and China. Historical records indicate that the Chinese Admiral Zheng He made seven historic expeditions to the Western Ocean (what is today the South China Sea and the Indian Ocean) between 1405–1433. While in the Persian Gulf during the fourth voyage (1414–1415), Zheng He encountered traders from the East African coasts of Mogadishu, Barawa, and Malindi. He then asked them to accompany him to China to pay tribute to the emperor, and they agreed (Levathes 1994, 140). During the fifth voyage, the treasure fleet, on arriving at Aden, sailed to the East African coast to return the emissaries from Mogadishu, Barawa, and Malindi back to their homes (Levathes 1994, 149). They were in Malindi in 1418. On leaving, two of their ships sunk in Lamu, which is 137 km northeast of Malindi. While many of the crew died, it is believed that about 20 men succeeded in reaching ashore. It is said that they then converted to Islam, married local women, and lived among the Swahili, assertions that were confirmed in 2002 when the aforementioned experts carried out DNA tests to determine whether indeed there were any Chinese descendants on the island. The DNA results positively identified six people as having Chinese ancestors — an aging woman, Baraka Badi Shee, and her three daughters and two sons. One of Baraka's daughters, Mwamaka Sharifu, was subsequently awarded a scholarship by the Chinese Government, and in 2005 she went to study Chinese Traditional Medicine in China.

In the novel, visitors from China accompanied by 'heritage experts' from the National Museum of Kenya visit Pate. After ascertaining that Munira's daughter, Ayaana, has Chinese heritage, they confer upon her the title of 'the Descendant' (Owuor 2019, 152–153). Soon after, Ayaana is sent to China as a state guest (Owuor 2019, 158, 171). She travels by ship, MV Qingrui, captained by Lai Jin who later becomes Ayaana's husband. She then enrols for a degree in Nautical

Science at Xiamen Maritime University. Throughout her university education, Ayaana keeps recalling the primary knowledge of the sea taught to her mainly by Pate's leading seafarer, Muhidin, the father she chose to replace her biological father of whom she knows nothing. Other Pate islanders who have mastered this traditional knowledge of the sea albeit to varying degrees are Mehdi the shipbuilder and Kitwana, his colleague.

My reading of the unique, personal, and intimate knowledges of the sea that Owuor represents in her novel builds on Hester Blum's (2010) argument that maritime studies ought to focus on the materiality of the sea, a concept that is also advocated for by Isabel Hofmeyr (2019) who argues that we need to engage with 'the materiality and the seaness of the sea' (2). What we need, Blum posits, is 'a practice of oceanic studies that is attentive to the material conditions and praxis of the maritime world, one that draws from the epistemological structures provided by the lives and writings of those for whom the sea was simultaneously workplace, home, passage, penitentiary, and promise' (2010, 670). Blum's work reminds us of seafarers like Haji Gora — the sailor, fisherman, and poet whose voice permeates Owuor's novel. She argues that acknowledging seafarers and exploring their lives as a critical part of oceanic studies 'allows us to perceive, analyse, and deploy aspects of the history, literature, and culture of the oceanic world that might otherwise be rendered obscure or abstract' (2010, 671). After all, a history of the sea is 'the story of those who have traversed it, who have inhabited its shores, and who, through the power of the imagination, have conjured its many meanings' (Moorthy and Jamal 2010, 1).

Sensuous Seascapes in Pate: A Conversation between Pate Islanders and the Sea

In *The Dragonfly*, the materiality of the sea is rendered visible particularly when one reads the text through the lens of polysensoriality, one of the four elements of geocriticism proposed by Bertrand Westphal (2011). Here, Westphal proposes human senses as a critical means of perception (2011, 131–136). He emphasises that people structure, define and express their experience of the spaces they inhabit through multiple senses (132–133), including, as Margaret Pearce (2008) posits, those of 'sight, hearing, taste, touch, and smell [as well as] other more abstract "senses" that are linked to intuition, place, time, and connection to the past, present, and future' (Westphal 2011, 114). This conglomeration of senses, Paul Rodaway (2002) argues, '[offers] important media through which space and time is experienced and understood' (36). Evidently, key characters in *The Dragonfly* possess a polysensory experience of the sea; the sea speaks to them through the senses of sight, touch, and hearing. In addition to and working together with these is an intuitive sense which allows the characters to, for example, converse with the sea, to read the sea, and to make meaning out of events in the ocean.

A conversation between the sea and Pate islanders is made possible by the ability of the ocean to send messages to the islanders be it through the sound of the waves, the movement of the winds, the humming of djinns, or even through the appearance of the water, and the islanders' capability to receive and decipher these messages. This intimate connection between the sea and the islanders speaks to intuitive and embodied knowledges of the sea common to shore folk in general. Among fishermen in Lamberts Bay on the South African coast, for example, exist knowledges of the ocean derived from 'rhythms and nuances of the sea that [take] a lifetime of sensitivity and observation to learn' (Rogerson 2015, 329). These intuitive knowledges include fishermen using their boat's rocking sensation to detect storms, and reading and feeling the kind of water they are in to sense where fish might be (Rogerson 2015, 328).

This lively nature of the sea which makes it possible for characters in Owuor's novel to speak with the ocean reveals animist characteristics that the islanders attach to the sea. In this case, the sea is enlivened by djinns who live in it — they sigh (Owuor 2019, 125), make murmuring cries at night (197, 362, 373), sob (203, 242), wail (241), murmur (293), roar (363), whisper (373), sing (373), chant (375), and howl (449). Beside the djinns, other mystical elements of the sea are also invoked. For example, the wind and the ocean are placed in conversation, in which the wind calls *'Hooooooo!'* and the ocean answers *'Whaaaaaa!'* (89), most likely announcing the creation of a wave, which occurs when the wind brushes against the surface of water. In another example, the waves call, and the winds respond (217). The waters of the ocean, too, are presented as living entities, so that they can enquire from people who enter it, *'Ni shi shei?' 'Who are you?'* (383, 386, 390, 392, 468). This lively nature of the ocean attends to animist thought which Harry Garuba (2003) defines as:

> [an] almost total refusal to countenance unlocalized, unembodied, unphysicalized gods and spirits. Animism is often simply seen as belief in objects such as stones or trees or rivers for the simple reason that animist gods and spirits are *located* and *embodied* in objects: the objects are the physical and material manifestations of the gods and spirits. (267, original emphasis)

In animism, spiritual meanings are attached to natural and ordinary objects, which means that in this case, the sea is a spirit world, and the djinns and mystical elements the gods and spirits that reside therein. It is to these beings that the islanders go for help, like Munira was willing to negotiate with the grey-feathered djinn to free her daughter Ayaana from the curse she inherited from her. The islanders had taken to calling Ayaana *Mwanaharamu*, the cursed child, and *Mwana kidonda,* child of the wound, a result of her being born out of wedlock. At the same time, it is these animated sounds and cries from these sea spirits that the islanders must ignore, lest they be lured like Muhidin was. Muhidin's son and Munira's husband, Ziriyab, is kidnapped while fishing at sea. For years, nothing is heard of him, and there seems to be no hope for his return — his wife, Munira, moves on and marries Muhidin, and they even have a daughter together, Abeerah. One night, however, djinns appear to Muhidin in a dream, but in the form of Ziriyab. Muhidin makes the mistake of listening to them. In this dream:

> Mehdi [Pate's shipbuilder and Muhidin's closest friend, while telling Ayaana about Muhidin's last days] would remember Muhidin saying, Ziriyab had been on a metal bed in a small room drenched in fierce light, so Muhidin could see that his entire body had become a wound. Muhidin had smelled the foul green pus of death within Ziriyab's slowing crashing heart. Tearing up, Ziriyab had said to him, 'My father, it is good you came. I am dying.' Muhidin said he had shaken his son, slapped him awake. 'No!' he had commanded. Ziriyab had then pointed. 'See my heart. It is rotting.' Muhidin had shouted, 'Is it a heart you need? Then take mine. It is large. It is enough for you.' And in the dream he had torn out his heart and shoved it into Ziriyab, and did not let go until that heart had started to beat inside Ziriyab's body. 'And you, Father, and you?' Ziriyab had apparently clung to him. Muhidin told Mehdi that he had informed Ziriyab that since he carried his heart now, he would have to live for him, too. (Owuor 2019, 370)

Two days after this dream, Muhidin, in the company of Mehdi's colleague, Kitwana, sets out to the sea, hoping to find and rescue Ziriyab. Unfortunately, Muhidin had answered the djinns in the dream, imagining he was talking to Ziriyab himself. As a result, neither he nor Kitwana return from the sea. Mehdi tells Ayaana that '[Muhidin] spoke of Ziriyab … Dreamed of his boy. In the dream, he said he had handed over his heart' (Owuor 2019, 421). This, Mehdi finally understands, is '[a] prophecy of sacrifice … How could we know? Would have told Kitwana to wait' (421). This implies that even if Mehdi or anyone else had known that Muhidin had sacrificed his soul for Ziriyab's well-being, they would not have been able to stop Muhidin from going to the sea; the best they could have done is to stop Kitwana from accompanying him. On the other hand, Ziriyab who was about to die (440), gets to live again and reappears in Pate soon after (446–447). He and Munira remarry towards the end of the novel.

From the ongoing discussion, it emerges that the sea is perhaps most materialised by the djinns who inhabit the ocean. It is with these beings that people engage the most. For instance, Ayaana and Munira are presented as imploring the djinns, and thereby the sea, to return Muhidin to them. When Ayaana hears that her chosen father Muhidin has disappeared into the sea, she is at first in denial, saying, 'Thank you. But my father is the ocean. Therefore, he does not drown. He is a wave. He is also the tide. He will return' (372). As days pass, however, Ayaana gets impatient, and asks Munira if Muhidin has returned, to which Munira answers, 'Not yet … We have petitioned the sea and its deities for mercy' (372). At this point, Ayaana decides to speak with the water. She sneaks out of class and heads to the ocean and 'the more she walked, the more she felt the sea come close to her, and if the sea was close to her, so was Muhidin' (373).

Unfortunately, her reading of the water shows no sign of Muhidin, for as she lifts her arms from the water, she does not hear the tingling sensation which would have assured her that Muhidin was alive and had heard her screaming for him (376). The irretrievability of Muhidin's soul is further captured in Ayaana's realisation that the watch Muhidin gave her as a parting gift when she went to China is dead, 'That watch. The *ping* ... has gone from it' (386), symbolising loss.

Ayaana's communion with the water reveals that speaking with the sea is a skill that requires one to carefully select the time and place for it. There are specific times that the sea, under the right conditions, is accessible, and can receive and send back messages. For instance, amid Ayaana's desperate attempts to speak with the water, '[o]nly later, after the sun dipped into the water, did Ayaana find the portal at the water's edge from which she could call out to Muhidin in a high cry that split winds and forced them into listening-waiting' (390). It also reveals how powerful the sea is, to an extent that the shorefolk revere it as they would a god. This is why when Ayaana is searching for Muhidin's soul in the sea, she 'informed both God and the sea that Muhidin was her heart, her spirit, her breath. She told God and the sea that they owed her his life' (390). The power of the sea is further illustrated by the fact that even when the sea is open and receives messages from those eager to find answers from it, it is not always that the sea responds, it does so at its own time. For example, an imam in Pate, while consoling Ayaana who has just arrived from China, tells her, 'The ocean is a cipher ... We can only wait' (415). In another example, Ayaana, upon returning to Pate, hires a search party for Muhidin, 'souls reading the water for clues of life' (420). Making no headway, Ayaana finally recalls the search. It would be over nine months before the sea finally answers back, for one day, '[a] fisherman, not one of the best, had hauled in an exceptionally bountiful catch. Among his miscellaneous sea bounty ... was a ruby ring that had last been seen on Muhidin's right ring finger. And the fisherman understood that the sea might have been speaking' (452). Thus, while Munira, Ayaana, and all of Pate's seamen spend months persuading the sea to release or reveal the fate of Muhidin, it is not until the sea is ready that Pate gets to know what befell Kitwana and Muhidin.

As hinted earlier, this sensuous seascape also manifests in the subtle ways in which the islanders can read events in the ocean. From experience, they read signs on water but also those on land, to predict what is about to happen in the sea. Outside of science, they have developed reliable systems of knowledge, largely based on intuition. For example, while conversing with Munira, Muhidin says that he 'noticed that the ants are carrying food into their nests', to which Munira responds, 'Storm', and Muhidin agrees that it is 'Likely' (78). Similarly, Nioreg and Delaksha, both passengers on MV Qingrui, the ship aboard which Ayaana is on the way to China, predict a storm. Nioreg says that there is going to be a 'storm in a few days', and when Delaksha asks him how he can tell, he replies, 'Wind on waves' (215). It appears that it takes great experience for one to own and hone this expertise. For example, eighteen months after Ziriyab and Munira's marriage, Ziriyab goes to do some fishing at sea. Unfortunately, there suddenly appears the historic 2004 Indian Ocean tsunami, which claimed over 200 000 lives and is understood to have been caused by an earthquake of magnitude 9.0 which lifted the sea floor by several metres (Bose 2006, 1). Ziriyab regrets that he had not been a fisherman long enough to be able to read the signs, for 'he would have known to read the action of fish that had abandoned their feeding grounds that day … He might have understood that he could not make it back to shore in time' (102). He ends up with his boat capsized, and it would be eight and half days before he could sight land again. This indigenous knowledge of the sea is learned through socialisation, so that as islanders grow, their knowledge and experience of the sea expands.

Notably, characters do not exhibit sensory experiences of the sea in isolation, but rather, as the novel's main character illustrates, this intuitive knowledge is to some extent blended with pragmatic knowledge. Owuor's decision to present intuitive practices alongside scientific knowledge calls attention to the fact that there are multiple ways of knowing, and people utilise them concurrently, not to forget that they serve the same purposes. For instance, Nautical Science, which Ayaana has gone to study in China, is to the maritime world what reading the tides, listening to the wind, and reading the stars is to the people and fishermen of Pate (286–287).

However, this intuitive knowledge is rarely noticed because widely accepted epistemologies often confine logic to what can be seen or measured (Garuba 2013, 44), and anything that falls outside this epistemic territory 'is made invisible, is excluded from the real and is actively disdained, even unnamed' (Vázquez 2011, 30). This has resulted in the exclusion of a great variety of knowledges since '[t]he real is not only what is observable or what makes cognitive sense; it is also the invisible, the emotional, the sentimental, the intuitive and the inexplicable' (Nyamnjoh 2017, 258). Therefore, Owuor uses the intimate relationship between Pate islanders and the sea to call attention to alternative epistemologies and thereby criticise the form of epistemicide caused by the stark binary between science and non-science.

When Ayaana goes to study in China, the novel at first presents her as being faced with a situation in which she has to shed all the primary senses in favour of science. She feels as though she would have to relinquish her feeling for water for the power of numbers, navigational compasses, Napier's rules, coordinates, and geopolitics (Owuor 2019, 287). This is yet another reminder that knowledge is hinged on power, and that some forms of knowledge have dominated others, and have required that people who are deemed powerless should subscribe to the knowledge system that is regarded as superior (Nyamnjoh 2017, 255). In the face of this new epistemology Ayaana is confronted with, however, she seems to be in favour of her traditional knowledge of the sea, which she learned from a tender age — by seven, she was searching for dragonflies in the lagoon by herself, and soon after, Muhidin had taught her how to read the water. She refuses to renounce her secret knowledge of the sea, but she keeps this to herself, lest she be deported (Owuor 2019, 288). Owuor uses Ayaana's initial resistance to science to demonstrate the sophisticated forms of knowledge that exist outside the frame of scientific paradigms. For example, when a typhoon occurs in Xiamen and catches people by surprise, Ayaana regrets that Mehdi was not there, for he would have read it (361). In other words, Owuor is saying that there are varied epistemologies for navigating the sea, and they are all valid and often complement each other. Interestingly, after Ayaana graduates with her degree in Nautical Science, and long after she has returned to Pate, she is still in possession of her primary senses of the sea. This could be Owuor's way of emphasising that the different knowledges of the sea need not displace each other, that they can coexist. In fact, the novel ends when Ayaana, a nautical scientist, is working with Mehdi, a Pate seafarer, in Mehdi's shipyard (422).

Indigenous Knowledges of the Sea as Requisite for Belonging to Pate

The local knowledges of the sea discussed above are in the novel presented as constituting a threshold of admission, acceptability, and belonging to Pate Island. In this section, I analyse how would-be islanders are expected to embrace and express these indigenous knowledges, lest they be locked out of the island. To illustrate this, I expound on how Owuor imagines the stages that would-be islanders undergo before they become part of Pate, a process that sounds much like what is believed to have happened with the 20 Chinese sailors in 1418 as hinted in the introduction:

> They were observed as they laughed at well-placed jokes; laughter was a test ... At some point in his Pate life, this person, now linked to a family and treated as such, would make a public pronouncement of Shahada: *Ash hadu anlla ilaha ilallah* ... Afterward, the new islander, giving his life over to the place, would, after taking a purifying bath to shed the skin of the past, adorn himself in a clean white garment and re-emerge, finally, at home. An island bride might be offered to him then. If the betrothal flowered, the visitor would take up a trade to sustain his home, and find himself written into the palimpsest that was Pate. (Owuor 2019, 69)

This allusion to Zheng He's expedition is further illustrated by journeys made by some of the characters in the novel, which invoke the grandiose encounters that the Kenyan coast had with the outside world centuries ago. Only two characters, both Chinese, make this transoceanic trip to Pate and after going through the process mentioned above, find a home on the island — Kitwana and Lai Jin. As part of their initiation into belonging to Pate, both get new names — Kitwana was formerly Mchina Nihao,[2] while Lai Jin is renamed Nahodha Jamal, a name given to him by Pate fishermen (466). 'Nahodha' is Kiswahili for 'Captain', a title that Lai Jin officially lost when his ship was seized and burned by Shanghai Accent, the Chinese merchant whose cargo Lai Jin dumped in the ocean after Lai Jin discovered that Shanghai Accent had tricked him into transporting illicit cargo disguised as scrap metal (250–253). His renaming by Pate fishermen cements his belonging to the seas. After getting a new name, Jamal pronounces the Shahada and thus officially converts to Islam, after which he cuts his hair short, takes a purifying bath, and adorns himself in a white garment (475). Islamised, he now belongs to God and Pate, and can marry a Pate woman to complete his assimilation. The novel ends with Jamal and Ayaana's wedding (480–481).

Ayaana embodies these Chinese links, seeing as she is not only a Chinese descendant, but also looks like one. When Kitwana encounters her for the first time, he is struck by how much 'she evoked for him something of a child of another China' (66). There is even a hint that the two look alike (113). Also, in the midst of her classmates in Xiamen, China —16 students from different maritime countries across Asia and the Middle east — Ayaana stands out for being taller and darker, but unmistakably appears to have 'familiar Asian looks' (280). Unlike the friendly accommodation of the Chinese castaways on Pate, Ayaana does not feel at home in China, despite her Chinese heritage. Ayaana's yearning for belonging awakens in her a desire to know her biological father. On three separate occasions when she calls her mother Munira, she asks who her father, 'the one of [her] blood' is, and where she can find him (279, 306, 397). She feels increasingly desolate, to the point when she decides that she will not stay in China because '[s]he was not Chinese' (387). She tells her mother, 'I am not Chinese, Ma-e, and I never shall be' (359). She finally concludes: 'This nation. I am not its descendant' (393), and plans her return home. When she arrives at the airport in Nairobi, she is confronted with 'Umerudi?', *You are back?* To which she responds 'Nimerudi', *I am back*, implying that she was meant to come back.

Contrasted with Ayaana's inability to fit in, in China, Kitwana and Lai Jin's transformation reveals the unique hospitality of Pate. At the same time, we have seen that their success is determined by their ability to live up to expectations set by the Pate islanders themselves. Therefore, the island does not just assimilate whoever approaches it. Rather, there are certain ways in which different people are evaluated to establish whether they deserve to form part of Pate, or if they should be turned away. Pate, as Owuor paints it, is a community of people who largely live in harmony with each other,[3] and who possess unique local knowledges about the sea, with which they coexist. For outsiders to be admitted to Pate, and in order for them to be granted their desire to belong to the island, they ought to exhibit qualities similar to those of the islanders. What underlies this possibility for Pate to open itself to these visitors is, of course, the nature of islands themselves as open and porous spaces (Stratford 2003, 495). Essentially, islands embody openness (Glissant 1989, 139), are permeable to travellers (DeLoughrey 2019, 6), and consist of 'people that defy territoriality' (Baldacchino 2008, 39). As I have mentioned, however, as much as this openness exists, so that knowledges from elsewhere and people from anywhere are allowed in, the visitors have to learn the local code should they want to stay longer, or permanently. The island, then, exhibits both inclusion as well as exclusion. For this reason, the image of the island is akin to that of the globe, whereby 'each isle might be read metonymically as the globe' (DeLoughrey 2007, 1). Concerning the figure of the island as world, which carries both the inside(r) and outside(r), and the accepted and the nonaccepted, Steinberg (2013) notes that:

> This representation serves modernity well, as it reproduces the idea that the world consists of, on the one hand, static terrestrial points on the 'inside' that may be settled, developed, and grouped into states and, on the other hand, aqueous points on the 'outside' that, due to the absence of properties that enable settlement and territorialization, may be written off as beyond society. (159–160)

Some of the people who approach Pate in the novel are welcomed, accepted, and assimilated, while others, those who lack the disposition associated with the island, are frowned at, rejected, and eventually sent away. Based on this, the novel presents three kinds of people on Pate Island, visitors and locals alike. First, '[t]here were those who, unknown even to themselves, belonged to the island and were covenanted to stay' (Owuor 2019, 68). A good example is Mehdi, Pate's shipbuilder and reader of the sea. Even Muhidin, his closest friend, fails to convince Mehdi to relocate to Pemba. Second, there were those 'who left, only to show up again years later' (68). These include Ziriyab who leaves and returns to Pate twice in the novel; Munira who also reappears in the novel twice, the first time with Ayaana and the second time with Abeerah, her daughter with Muhidin; and Muhidin who travels in and out of Pate, until the sea in Pate finally converts him to a martyr. Finally, there are those who 'scowled, sulked, scolded, and stipulated that the island transform itself for them. Invariably, the right winds swooped in to sweep these away' (68). These will either be visitors who take advantage of Pate's hospitality or Pate islanders themselves who disrupt the peace on the island.

In the first category (visitors who take advantage of Pate's generosity) are people like Fazul the Egyptian and Wa Mashriq. Both are Muslim terrorists who tried to recruit Pate islanders as Mujahideen, unfortunately, with some level of success. Fazul succeeds in converting seven of Pate's seamen, and also tries to convert Ayaana to a Mujahidat, but fails (69–77). He had taken advantage of Ayaana's loneliness, anguish, desperation, and lovelessness, and had made her believe that if she became God's little martyr, her mother Munira would be freed of her curse and shame (71–73). Muhidin rescues Ayaana by confronting and fighting with Fazul, an altercation that causes Fazul to leave Pate (77). However, it is Wa Mashriq that nearly succeeded in completing the mission Fazul had started (139–142). He promises Munira 1.5 million shillings in exchange for Ayaana, and Munira even accepts a deposit of seventy-five thousand (133). It is only later, when Wa Mashriq tries to rape Ayaana, that Munira changes her mind, and scalds Wa Mashriq with hot water (141). Muhidin then hires a team of pirates to ensure that Wa Mashriq's and Fazul's boats do not approach the East African coastline again (423). In contrast, an example of Pate islanders themselves who the sea sweeps away is Suleiman, Ayaana's classmate and constant bully. He does not return from the Emirates where he had gone to get higher education. Rather, he gets lured into the Syrian Islamic Liberation Front (294), and the narrative hints at his death in action (456–457). The terrorist activities that Fazul, Wa Mashriq, and Suleiman are engaged in reveal the diverse networks of Muslim fundamentalism that to some extent underlie contemporary Islamic cultures of the Indian Ocean world.

From these illustrations, Owuor makes it clear that while all are welcome on Pate Island, who gets to stay is determined by the visitors' resolve to abide by the host's code of conduct. It requires them to cultivate and maintain a good relationship with other islanders and with the sea. The first two categories of people are welcome on the island because they are able to coexist with the sea. They respect and protect it. Like Lai Jin, they guard against selfish and exploitative uses of the sea. After Lai Jin discovers that Shanghai Accent had tricked him, and that what he was carrying in MV Qingrui was not scrap metal, but illicit cargo, wildlife, he tosses the containers into the sea (250). He had been instructed to transfer this cargo to another ship which he was to meet in the high seas at night. He and his crew then invent a storm which is supposed to have threatened to capsize the ship, '[forcing] the captain to select containers to dump overboard' (253). Unfortunately, Lai Jin's trick is eventually discovered, and he gets stiffly punished for it — he is sentenced to 13 months in prison and his ship is seized and burned.

The third category of people, by contrast, are unwelcome because they have proven to be selfish and dangerous. They have caused disturbance on the island, and their refusal to share in the norms and values cherished on the island demands that they be eliminated. Thus, the island, depending on how people behave within and around it, will either include or exclude them. At the same time, no matter how much of an islander one might be, one has to consistently uphold the local code, because Pate islanders themselves also risk being kicked off the island, like Suleiman was.

Conclusion

This paper has brought two things to light — the centrality of the sea to the lives of shore folk and seafarers, in the novel represented by Pate islanders and Muhidin respectively; and a sensuous and material seascape derived from indigenous knowledges of the sea that shore folk possess. The dominance and centrality of the sea in *The Dragonfly* is shown whereby the sea is constructed not as a passive body in and around which people act, but rather as an active entity in the ecosystem. In fact, the sea is given power to influence people's actions and movements, and even to determine or twist their fate. Throughout the novel, the sea is responsible for bringing people together as it is for tearing them apart, for bringing them waves of happiness just as it also washes grief to their shores. As such, the same winds that bring visitors like Kitwana and Lai Jin, are the same ones that sweep away unwanted ones, like Suleiman the bully, and Fazul and Wa Mashriq, the Muslim terrorists who tried to sacrifice Ayaana, Munira's daughter, as a Mujahidat.

These two issues are reflected in the style in which the novel is written. The multiple approaches to reading the sea, coupled with the hospitality of Pate which allows the island to accommodate diverse peoples and cultures, reminds the reader of the major character, Muhidin, who has mastered many languages of the seas including Kiswahili, English, Portuguese, Arabic, and Persian. Phrases and sayings from different traditions are also incorporated into the text. In particular, Kiswahili, Arabic, and Chinese words and phrases populate the text. Owuor's selection of these languages mirrors the different communities the novel brings together: there are the Swahili of the Lamu Archipelago; the Muslim population who are the majority on the Kenyan coast; and the two groups of Chinese found in the novel, Ayaana's ancestors from 1418 and the arrivals in the twenty-first century, like Lai Jin and Mzee Kitwana (Mchina Nihao). The coexistence of these languages and their ability to capture and translate the materiality of the sea attests to the openness and hospitality of Pate described above.

Notes

1. Other settings include China where Ayaana, the novel's protagonist, goes to study; the Indian Ocean across which Ayaana voyages in MV Qingrui, captained by Lai Jin who later becomes Ayana's husband; and Turkey, where Koray Terzioglu, Ayaana's classmate and boyfriend, takes Ayaana for the holidays, for her to meet his family.
2. Mchina Nihao is a nickname derived from Kitwana's origin (Mchina) and the Chinese greeting (nǐ hǎo). Kitwana's own names are not given in the text.
3. However, underlying this semblance of harmony and hospitality is gender conflict, as Pate imposes tougher conditions on women. Owuor uses Munira to reveal the challenges that female islanders have to endure. For instance, when Munira and her daughter Ayaana first appear on the island, after Munira's two-and-a-half years' disappearance, the islanders receive her coldly. Pate is not ready to accept an unwed mother, and when Munira declines an arranged marriage, her family disowns her and immediately relocates to Zanzibar, abandoning Munira and her daughter (2019, 22). Also, Ayaana inherits her mother's faults, for she is soon referred to as *Mwanaharamu*, the cursed child, and *Mwana kidonda,* child of the wound.

Acknowledgements

I thank my PhD supervisors, Prof. Tina Steiner and Dr Uhuru Phalafala, Stellenbosch University, for their comments on the chapter of my dissertation from which this paper is extracted. I also thank Mingqing Yuan, University of Bayreuth, for productive discussions we had on Owuor's novel.

Disclosure Statement

No potential conflict of interest was reported by the author.

ORCID iD

Jauquelyne Kosgei http://orcid.org/0000-0002-0359-556X

References

Baldacchino, G. 2008. "Studying Islands: On whose terms?: Some epistemological and methodological challenges to the pursuit of Island Studies." *Island Studies Journal*. 3 (1): 37–56.

Blum, H. 2010. "The Prospect of Oceanic Studies." *PMLA*. 125 (3): 670–677.

Bose, S. 2006. *A Hundred Horizons: The Indian Ocean in the age of global empire*. Cambridge: Harvard University Press.

DeLoughrey, E. 2019. *Allegories of the Anthropocene*. Durham and London: Duke University Press.

DeLoughrey, E. 2007. *Routes and Roots: Navigating Caribbean and Pacific island literatures*. Honolulu: Hawai'i University Press.

Garuba, H. 2003. "Explorations in Animist Materialism: Notes on reading/writing African literature, culture, and society." *Public Culture*. 15 (2): 261–285.

Garuba, H. 2013. "On animism, Modernity/Colonialism, and the African Order of Knowledge: Provisional reflections." In *Contested Ecologies: Dialogues in the South on nature and knowledge*, ed. L. Green, 42–51. Cape Town: HSRC Press.

Glissant, E. 1989. *Caribbean Discourse: Selected essays*. Charlottesville: Virginia UP.

Hofmeyr, Isabel. 2019. "Literary Ecologies of the Indian Ocean." *English Studies in Africa*. 62 (1): 1–7.

Levathes, L. 1994. *When China Ruled the Seas: The Treasure Fleet of the Dragon Throne 1405-1433*. New York: Simon & Schuster.

Moorthy, S. and A. Jamal. 2010. "Introduction: New conjunctures in maritime imaginaries." In *Indian Ocean Studies: Cultural, social, and political perspectives*, edited by S. Moorthy and A. Jamal, 1–31. New York: Routledge.

Nyamnjoh, F.B. 2017. "Incompleteness: Frontier Africa and the Currency of Conviviality." *Journal of Asian and African Studies*. 52 (3): 253–270.

Owuor, Y.A. 2014. *'Dragonfly Monsoon' and Imagined Oceans: In search of poem-maps of the Swahili Seas*. Brisbane: The University of Queensland.

Owuor, Y.A. 2018. "In Search of Poem-Maps of the Swahili Seas: Three Sea Poems by Haji Gora Haji." *Eastern African Literary and Cultural Studies*. 4 (3–4): 164–178.

Owuor, Y.A. 2019. *The Dragonfly Sea*. New York: Knopf.

Pearce, M.W. 2008. "Framing the Days: Place and narrative in Cartography." *Cartography and Geographic Information Science*. 35 (1): 17–32.

Rodaway, P. 2002. *Sensuous Geographies: Body, sense and place*. London & New York: Routledge.
Rogerson, J.M. 2015. "Being Heard: Thinking through different versions of rationality, epistemological policing and dissonances in marine conservation." *Marine Policy*. 60: 325–330.
Steinberg, P.E. 2013. "Of Other Seas: Metaphors and materialities in maritime regions." *Atlantic Studies*. 10 (2): 156–169.
Stratford, E. 2003. "Flows and Boundaries: Small island discourses and the challenge of sustainability, community and local environments." *Local Environment*. 8 (5): 495–499.
Vázquez, R. 2011. "Translation as Erasure: Thoughts on Modernity's Epistemic Violence." *Journal of Historical Sociology*. 24 (1): 27–44.
Westphal, B. 2011. *Geocriticism: Real and fictional spaces*. New York: Palgrave Macmillan.

Surviving the Genocide: The Singularity of Suffering in Yvonne Owuor's "Weight of Whispers"

Edgar Fred Nabutanyi

ABSTRACT

Although Theodor Adorno famously declared in 1983 that to write a poem after Auschwitz is barbaric, profound acts of horror have inspired many literary masterpieces. The 1994 Rwandan genocide is no exception, having motivated some of Africa's literary gems. While a huge archive of Rwandan genocide fiction easily and conveniently slips into the binaries of evil/good and Tutsi/Hutu, which have become default tropes of writing about this African traumatic reality, Kenyan writer Yvonne Adhiambo Owuor sets her short story in Nairobi and after the genocide in order to offer alternative insights into the less explored aspect of genocide fiction — post-genocide suffering. Whereas the Kuseremanes ironically assume that they have escaped the ghost of the genocide when they relocate to Nairobi, Owuor's spatial and temporal registers demonstrate how dislocation and innuendoes of their complicity in the genocide catalyses the family's inordinate suffering. She invests her short story with implicitly nuanced and subtle techniques that forcefully foreground the point that the Kuseremanes might have escaped the horrors of the genocide such as mass murder and rape by relocating to Nairobi, but they are fated to endure inordinate suffering because of genocide induced dislocation and societal rupture.

Introduction

Yvonne Owuor is one of the newest and freshest voices in East African writing, whose winning of the Caine Prize for African writing in 2003 has firmly cemented her position in the East African Literary canon, which is perhaps best exemplified by her nuanced exploration of genocidal suffering in "Weight of Whispers". Although Owuor (2006) does not mention the word genocide in the entire length of her text, the short story is understood as a genocide tale because of several textual insinuations. The passages: 'two presidents who died when a missile launched from the land forced their plane down,' (7) 'all has been cleansed,' (11) and the protagonist's name and physical appearance 'Boniface Louis R

Kuseremane' that are quintessentially Rwandan (13) place "Weight of Whispers" within the genocide literary archive. The above argument is reinforced by critics such as JKS Makokha (2011), Marie Kruger (2009) and Stephen Derwent Partington (2006), who have variously read the short story as a tale about the Rwandan genocide. While "Weight of Whispers" is recognisably a Rwandan genocide narrative, in this article, I explore how Owuor uses the genocide as a backdrop to an investigation of the pain that surfaces when someone's world is turned upside down.

While many writers who write about the Rwandan genocide focus on the horror of what is popularly known as the 100 days of madness, Owuor's "Weight of Whispers" dramatizes the post genocide suffering. The storyline of the short story traces the plight of a middle-class Rwandan family as it struggles to survive the harshness of exile and the ghosts of the genocide that they wrongly assume they had left in Rwanda. Owuor's short story skilfully deploys the metaphor of peeling to illustrate how under the inhospitable location of Nairobi and innuendos of their complicity in the genocide, the Kuseremanes are stripped of their facade of respectability, affluence and identity to reveal the corporeality of their pain. The above observation reminds us of Martha Nussbaum's postulation that the role of narrative literature in public reasoning is to make us understand the circumstances of someone we are normally unaware. Owuor's documentation of the Kuseremanes' pain forces readers to imagine the inordinate suffering that survivors of the genocide are subjected. This elevates post-genocidal suffering beyond statistical footnotes to the Rwandan genocide. This is because Owuor spotlights an aspect of the genocide that is often ignored in public discourses of this episode in African history.

The suffering that the Kuseremanes are immersed reminds us of Cyprian Ekwensi's (1976) *Survive the Peace.* The novel's exploration of the trials and tribulations that a former journalist during the Biafran war goes through in his quest to reunite and rebuild his family after the Nigerian civil war underlines the incomprehensive pain survivors of conflicts undergo. The protagonist's observation that post-civil war suffering is incomparable to the violence and suffering he had witnessed at the height of the civil war underscores the novel's title — *Survive the Peace.* This is because surviving the peace is more challenging than surviving the war. Although *Survive the Peace* and "Weight of Whispers" document different conflicts and at different moments in African history, I argue that they are comparable in as far as they elucidate the unexpected trauma that survivors of mass violence have to deal with in the aftermath of the conflicts.

Although "Weight of Whispers" has attracted considerable critical attention, most scholars offer a geopolitical reading of the short story. For example, Marie Kruger argues that Owuor's short story delivers 'a powerful critique of the modern nation state, its desires for a political opportune order, its monopoly of violence and its construction of privileged and disenfranchised categories of identity' (2009,14). In the above passage, Kruger highlights the enduring paradox of the African modern state as depicted in Owuor's text. While its citizens desire a political order that is empowering, the postcolonial African state is constructed in such a way that at any moment the identity of its citizens falls under two categories, namely those who are privileged and those who are disenfranchised. In fact, it is plausible to argue that these identity polarities — privilege and disenfranchisement — are always in flux. Kruger eloquently demonstrates how the Kuseremanes effortlessly segue between positions of privilege and disenfranchisement in the short story. The question that Kruger's reading does not fully ponder is the price that some have to pay as they oscillate between identities of privilege and marginalisation in moments of socio-political disruptions in the African postcolonial state.

JKS Makokha is another Owuor critic who privileges the rupture of the postcolonial state in his reading of "Weight of Whispers." He reads the Kuseremanes' exile and its attendant suffering as the manifestation of the dysfunctional African state and its identity politics. He argues that the short story is 'one about good and evil, injustice and betrayal, love and loss, about the mere struggle of living — of existence in the context of contemporary ethnicity-laced postcolonial society. The fate of the Kuseremane family in the Kenyan exile could almost be adapted to another family from another country in another exile' (2011, 87). Like Kruger before him, Makokha focusses on identity and socio-political disruptions in his reading of this text. For Makokha, the Kuseremanes' exile is not only a consequence of ethnic and identity politics that is characteristic of the postcolonial African state, but it is also a template of the rupture of identity politics. This perhaps explains why he argues that the Kuseremanes' exile is symptomatic of any and all African exile stories. From this perspective, it is plausible to note that although Makokha's focus on identity politics is a valid and persuasive interpretation of the short story, it nevertheless overshadows the thematic relevance of the singularity of human suffering that Owuor's text also brilliantly showcases. Although Makokha should be applauded for divorcing Owuor's short story from the simple binaries associated with Rwandan genocide literature, and by linking the text to the wider political crisis in Africa, nevertheless, his analysis does not go further enough to focus on the corporeality of suffering of African exile families like the Kuseremanes.

Ethnicity as an anchor of the dystopia of the African postcolonial state is also the focus of Stephen Derwent Partington's article: "Making Us Make Sense of Genocide." Partington argues that "Weight of Whispers" is a pessimistic story that traces the suffering of the Kuseremanes in exile. He proceeds to argue that the regression of the Kuseremane family illustrates the 'issues of postcolonial identity [...] in the context of contemporary Kenya and the wider Great Lakes Region' (2006, 110). He concludes with the observation that the text is 'an extraordinary and an extraordinarily innovative piece of postcolonial fiction [...] regarding some of the most pressing, fundamental and immediate issues of the time and the region' (2006, 121). It is true to argue that "Weight of Whispers" provides profound insights into the geopolitical issues in the

Great Lakes Region and issues occasioned by the 1994 Rwandan genocide. Thus, I agree with the essence of Partington's reading of "Weight of Whispers" as a geopolitical analysis of the intersection between identity, ethnicity and the violence of the postcolonial state.

Admittedly, the above-reviewed critics offer persuasive interpretations of Owuor's short story that I intend to build on by arguing for an alternative reading. While Kruger, Makokha and Partington attentively treat the pain of the Kuseremane as an allegory of the rupture of the postcolonial African state, I argue that Owuor's short story also weaves a story of personal tragedy that inevitably arises when individuals are dislocated due to mass violence. Her depiction of the singularity of suffering that the Kuseremanes undergo offers an alternative version of genocidal violence. The tale of how the Kuseremanes escape genocidal mass murder and rape only to suffer the indignities of exile utilises linguistic tools for the depiction of pain (Van Alphen 1999, 27). Owuor's register forces us to 'bear witness' to and to 'face the horror' (Douglas 2008, 149) of the awful suffering that the Kuseremanes endure in exile. Owuor's register of pain recalls Partington's argument that the protagonist in "Weight of Whispers" uses the 'present tense to create an immediacy that enables us read his disorientation at the same time as he experiences it' (2006, 120). Partington's main point in the above passage is that Owuor's narrative technique is crucial to our understanding of her text because it foregrounds the urgency of the protagonist's pain. I agree with Partington's assessment that Owuor deploys a language suitable for disclosing pain. However, I go further to argue that her register coheres with her plot, focalisation and characterisation to showcase the horrors of surviving the genocide only to be devastated by the inequities of exile.

The Burden of Survival

"Weight of Whispers" is a story about the dislocation of an upper-class Rwandan family at the start of the genocide to the Kenyan capital Nairobi. What the head of the family, Boniface R Kuseremane, ironically treats as a minor irritation of transiting through Kenya to his aristocratic connections in Europe and America turns out to be the family's worst nightmare. Pitied against the intractably corrupt Kenyan bureaucracy, uncaringly hypocritical international community and unfaithful friends and acquaintances (one could argue his acquaintances are frightened to associate with him on account of the rumours of his involvement in the genocide), the Kuseremanes' life rapidly and irrevocably disintegrates with catastrophic consequences for all the family members. This is symbolically reflected in the fact that starting from the Nairobi Hilton Hotel, they soon relocate to a one-roomed shack in River Road. This movement mimics the peeling away of the family's facades of opulence and respectability as it moves from the centre (symbolised by the Nairobi Hilton) to the periphery (symbolised by the one roomed shack in River Road).

The short story's theme of suffering is signalled by the adjective 'weight' in its title. The significance of the title statement to the text's theme of trauma is signalled by Kuseremane's confession to Professor George Nsibiriwa that their 'name is on the list' (47). The reaction of the Nsibiriwas — they hastily abandon the family — gestures not only to the burden of being pariahs accused of participation in a grievously heinous crime of genocide, but perhaps it also explains the family's suffering. It is arguable that Kuseremane's alleged support for the genocide is a reasonable explanation for the unanswered letters, unhelpful acquaintances and the indifferent monarchies in exile. Marked as guilty for orchestrating the genocide, it is understandable that no one wants to associate with or help them. This is because doing so is to mark oneself as a genocide sympathiser. If one were to read the adjective 'weight' in the title as the burden or affliction, then, the title references the suffering of the Kuseremanes on account of the rumours that link them to the planning and execution of the genocide. The title can also be read as signalling the hardships that the Kuseremanes undergo as they attempt to navigate the treacherous terrain of exile as they endeavour to relocate to the West. My reading of "Weight of Whispers" as trauma fiction focuses on the content (incidents in the plot that unveil both physical and psychological pain) and form (how the narrative technique such as the present tense, first person narrator, and especially the seamless segueing between the first person and the detachedly somnambulistic third person narrator) mimic the suffering of the family.

The Kuseremanes' physical and psychological trauma reminds us of Geoffrey Hartman's postulation that on the poetic or figurative level, trauma fiction 'may correspond to two types of cognition' (1995, 536) — the event (content) and the symptoms of the event (form). Hartman's postulation resonates with Anne Whitehead's question of whether 'trauma itself is content or form' (2004, 162). Both Hartman and Whitehead agree that trauma fiction is expressed as both content and form. While traumatic content is the painful experiences of the characters, traumatic form is a narrative stance that resembles the disclosure of traumatic experiences. The Hartman-Whitehead template of trauma fiction uncannily dovetails neatly into the plot, style and subject matter of "Weight of Whispers." For example, "Weight of Whispers" is full of scenes that depict the singularity of the Kuseremanes' suffering. These incidents portray the psychological humiliation and physical distress that they endure in Nairobi at the hands of different people.

The case in point is Boniface R Kuseremane's unlawful detention and the 'confiscation' of his property by Kenyan Police Officers. The above scene underlines two important points about Kuseremane's suffering. First, the incident nodes to his physical pain that is exemplified by the actions of the Police Officers who hit his head and twist his goatee. Second, the scene gestures to psychological torture of Kuseremane as underlined by the passage: 'later on much later on I will wonder what makes it possible for one man to hit another man for no reason other than the fact that he can' (7). The physical and psychological pain noted above showcases how the intersection between power and avarice of the Police Officers symbolises the suffering of dislocated people. The Police Officers literally erase Kuseremane's identity, memory, dignity and agency because of his disenfranchisement as a non-Kenyan citizen and an underclass. The alleged 'confiscation' of mementos such as the ring that marks him as a prince or the picture of his family that symbolise his manhood erases his agency and identity. This is confounded by the fact that he is helpless and powerless to do anything about his humiliation. This perhaps explains why he poses the rhetorical question 'but to be human is to be intrinsically, totally, resolutely good. Is it not?' (11) The question tag 'is it not' is significant because it simultaneously suggests a fact of life — human beings are supposed to be good — but also underscores puzzlement regarding how unfairly the Police Officers treat him. Kuseremane's rhetorical question accentuates his pain on account of the avarice and uncontrolled power of the Police Officers that turn him into a helpless victim.

The erasure of Kuseremane's agency and dignity is further depicted in his confrontations with the Immigration Officer and the Indian Pawn shop owner. As a former prince, diplomat and scholar, it can be argued that Kuseremane is used to or expects some degree of deference from ordinary people. However, his engagement with these two accentuates his depreciated social status. This is because they treat him in a manner that reduces him to a nonentity as the two passages below demonstrate. While the Indian Lady does not allow him to complain, asking rather loudly 'why do you let takataka to come in nee' (18), the Immigration Office laughs at him loudly when Kuseremane tells him about his PhD 'Ati PhD. PhD gani' (33). In both cases the cruelty of these characters towards Kuseremane is motivated by greed. By reducing him to a nonentity, it becomes simple for them to easily cheat and/or exhort money from him. The action of the two showcases how the erosion of Kuseremane's self-worth intersects with the inordinate power that other people have over him to subject him to psychological pain. By highlighting how far he has fallen, the text emphasises his suffering that is scripted in his transformation into nothing, or 'rubbish' if one were to paraphrase the Indian Lady's words.

The corrosion of the family's dignity and self-worth is further reinforced by their treatment at the European and American embassies in Nairobi. While the Europeans camouflage their refusal to grant the family visas, the Americans are openly hostile to the family's visa applications. This is underscored by two passages that describe the embassies' response to their visa applications. First, Kuseremane says that the Europeans process their visa applications 'until [he sees] they will be processed unto eternity' (18). Second, he describes the American officer in charge of visa applications thus: '[she] folds her papers, bangs them on the table and frowns as if I have wasted her time. She tosses my passport out of her little window into my hands that are outstretched, a supplication on an altar of disbelief' (20). The two passages further highlight the suffering of the Kuseremanes. Whether it is the condescending aloofness and hypocrisy of the Europeans or the unprecedented rudeness of the Americans, their actions translate into inordinate suffering for the depicted family. I argue that the indifference and dehumanising treatment that the family is subjected coagulates into agony and hopelessness that heightens its sense of abjection. The abjection is metonymically scripted by Kuseremane's posture of 'outstretched hands' which he describes as 'a supplication at the altar of disbelief' (20). While the wretchedness of his condition is infused in the paradoxical statement 'supplication on the altar of disbelief,' what pulls at the chords of our empathy is the distressed act of reaching out for help, empathy or mere understanding only to be rudely turned away.

Kuseremane's treatment in the above passages reminds us of Kimberly Nance's observation that 'the goal of testimonial narratives is not only to educate readers about injustice, but to persuade those readers to act' (2006, 19). If Nance considers trauma fiction as playing an educational and activism function, then, it is arguable that "Weight of Whispers" does more than allegorise the ruptures of postcolonial African states. It underlines the singularity of suffering of the depicted family that is exploited and abused by different categories of Kenyans. It is no wonder that a few pages later the elliptic narrator informs us that 'it is odd, the sounds that make a grown-up man weep [...] one morning in which the sun shone pink, I found that a certain sorrow had become a tenant of my body and weighed down' (29). In a society where masculinity is equated to hardness and where 'softness' is frown at, for a man, a head of a family and a prince to breakdown and cry is a manifestation of total despondency, even if the crying is done in secrecy. This is emphasised by the oscillation between the first person and the omniscient narrator in this and similar scenes in the text. The use of the adjectival phrase 'a grown-up man weep' and the personification 'sorrow renting his body' articulated in the third person perspective underlines the intensity of his pain. While the tears are a register that expresses an agony that ordinary speech is incapable of disclosing, the third person narrator signals his need to distance himself from the excessive pain of this episode. That he mourns in silence also suggests that his pain is outside the scope of his register. This is an elliptic invitation of the reader to inhabit his space in order to attempt to understand what it means and/or feels to be abused and tortured the way he has been.

The Kuseremanes' pain brings to mind Lauren Berlant's argument in "Introduction: Compassion (and Withholding)" that 'compassion is a term denoting privilege: the sufferer is over there' (2004, 3). The essence of Berlant's argument above is the impossibility of a witness to fully understand the suffering or the pain of another person. This is because as witnesses we are far removed from the pain that the Kuseremanes are going through in the short story. Readers as witnesses cannot readily comprehend the pain of a man who cannot care for his family because of circumstances beyond his control. The secret tears and the sorrow that has rent space in his being are what draws our empathy without any idea if we can empathise enough. How can we commiserate sufficiently with a grown-up man who is reduced to silent tears because he cannot support his family? Is this the kind of content that Geoffrey Hartman in "Shoah and Intellectual Witness" says puts us in an uncomfortable place of spectators where we 'are exposed, at one and the same time, to the trauma and anxiety of not empathising enough' (1998, 42). Perhaps as Hartman insightfully suggests, Kuseremane's suffering dovetails neatly into the dreadful content that readers cannot fully understand nor relate to nor make sense of.

Anne Whitehead argues that 'trauma can be presented in a narrative but only in a literary form which departs from conventional linear sequence' (2004, 6). There is no doubt that style of "Weight of Whispers" successfully documents the physical and psychological pain that the Kuseremanes' negotiate to survive on Nairobi's streets. Therefore, the significance of "Weight of Whispers" as trauma narrative is imbued in how its disjointed structure coheres with the present tense and the seamless segueing between the first person and a detachedly somnambulistic third person narrator to perfectly mimic the pain of the Kuseremanes. For example, by frequently referring to himself in the third person across the short story, Kuseremane signals his inability to make sense of or articulate his pain. It can also be read as an artistic invitation for the reader to place him/herself in Kuseremane's shoes to appreciate his pain. It can also be argued that the switching between the narrators is an artistic mimicry of a mind that has rejected pain or one that has created an inviolable space that pain cannot intrude into. This is particularly true because the segueing between the two narrators is frequent at the height of Kuseremane's despondency as highlighted by his emasculation and subsequent loss of his family.

Kuseremane's despondency and emasculation is further accentuated by the sexual harassment of his fiancée and sister. The omniscient narrator observes that the family decides to register as refugees in order to locate to Canada when it is abandoned by its acquaintances such as the Nsibiriwas because they are on 'the list' of genocide collaborators. However, the ultimatum given to his fiancée and sister, namely, to be 'examined by the officials at their homes for a night' (51) is an enormous price that the women have to pay for the family to relocate to Canada. Given that the examination of the women by the officials is shorthand for sexual harassment, one can understand how emasculating this is for Kuseremane. The pain of emasculation is underscored in the passage: 'annals of war decree that conquest of landscapes is incomplete unless the vanquisher's women are 'taken'. Where war is crudest, the women are discarded, afterwards for their men to find' (51–52). While this can be read as tacit approval of the sacrifice and a philosophical justification of the exploitation, the actions that follow tell a different story. In fact, it can be argued that this statement signals an involuntary blockage of the awful reality of renting out one's fiancée and sister to sex predators in exchange for visas. His action of rationalising the exploitation is a philosophical wishing away or blocking out the harsh reality that he has sold his women folk into sexual slavery for the sake of the family.

It is understandable that his world crashes and crumbles when he realises the steep price that his fiancée and sister have to pay to save the family. This is because the prostitution of his sister and fiancée symbolises the death of the family and his manhood. Here, we recall the intertextuality of his mother's mournful tune that hums in the background of this scene. The tune from a song 'new widows sing when the body of their dead spouse is laid on the bier,' (51) gestures to the symbolic, if not, the literal disintegration or death of the family. In a patriarchal setting of the text, when one's sister and fiancée prostitute themselves to save the family, then for all purposes and intents, the man of the family is literally and symbolically dead. This is because their sacrifice symbolises the failure and/or inability of the man of the family to protect and provide for his family. It also acts as a preamble to the deaths that will break up the family after the women stain its honour.[1]

The intense pain arising from Kuseremane's complete emasculation is illustrated by his ineffectually violent actions. He tears the visas into small pieces and strikes at both his sister and fiancée. The detachedly somnambulistic narrative posture signals Kuseremane's anguish in this part of the text. It also reveals the extreme pain that the narrator is unable to comprehend, let alone explain. Chi-Chi's statement that 'but we shall live … chéri we shall live … we shall live' (60) notwithstanding, the steep price the women have to pay, ironically translate into the death and disintegration of the family. This is because the exchange of sexual favours for the visas ruptures the dignity that has so far held the family together. This is scripted in Kuseremane's somnambulistic actions in the passage: 'I watched from a far […] as the tall man tears the papers to shreds. I am curious about the weeping woman with her shorn hair […] I see the tall black man lift his hand up right up and bring it crashing into the back of the girl' (60). Kuseremane's ineffectual, but violent actions signal the disintegration of the family as symbolised by Chi-Chi's miscarriage and death. It is arguable that Chi-Chi, who still sucks at her thumb, is too fragile to survive the horror and the pain of exile and the genocide.

Chi-Chi and Agnethe-mama die because women's bodies and sexuality are marked as prizes for the victorious and powerful on the one hand. On the other hand, they are scapegoats for an emasculated patriarchy that cannot protect the honour of the family. This perhaps explains why the matriarchy of the family gives up life and survival when it becomes apparent that the women's bodies and sexuality has to be exchanged for the welfare of the family. This is indicated by her decision to sell her wedding ring for the family to survive (53). Given the socio-religious value attached to a wedding ring, (especially the fact that a ring in Christian marriages symbolise a lifelong commitment scripted in the vow 'till death do us part'), it can be argued that alongside the widow's tune she frequently hums, the selling of the ring signals her symbolic death. It is also important to note that she spends her last days in the garden. This action seems to suggest that she is surrounding herself with as much life as she can as her own life ebbs out. It is no wonder that her health deteriorates soon afterwards (56–65). The fact that she dies on the eve of their departure to Canada significantly speaks to the complete disintegration of the family. Without its matriarchy to keep it together and its paterfamilias abused and debased by the vagaries of exile, the story ends in the family's complete rupture. While Lune will depart for Canada that evening, Kuseremane will, in a deranged obstinate state, ostensibly mourn his mother's death and celebrate his second birth: 'thus began the first day of my second life' (68). Like the proverbial phoenix, the new Kuseremane emerges out of the ashes of extreme suffering and degradation on the streets of Nairobi.

Kuseremane's rebirth under the fire of pain, emasculation and rejection on the Kenyan streets reminds us of Anne Whitehead's argument that 'trauma emerges as that which, at the very moment of its reception, registers as a non-experience, causing conventional epistemologies to falter' (Whitehead 2004, 5). The essence of Whitehead's argument is that trauma is unrecognisable as trauma when it occurs. I bring this point to my exploration of Kuseremane's final disintegration as brilliantly scripted by his inability to recall his name: 'what is my name? I frown. What is my name?' (38). Kuseremane's failure to recall his name is reinforced by a flashback-cum-anecdote of a Sierra Leonean Leeds-educated sociologist now turned hawker that he meets in Amsterdam (38–41). Kuseremane's fate is comparable to that of this unfortunate man in the anecdote, because exile has erased their identity and agency that a name symbolises. It is instructive that he muses that 'in exile we cower our head so that we do not see in the mirror of another's eyes, what we suspect that our precarious life rests entirely on the whim of another's tolerance of our presence' (41). That exile has cowered and broken him is beyond question as the loss and disintegration of his family eloquently suggest. Left alone, the real impact of his suffering hits him with the profound realisation that the veneer of prince, diplomat, scholar, world citizen has been erased, leaving a naked corporeality of a suffering soul.

Thus, it can be argued that Owuor's innovatively affective narrative texture and register transforms Kuseremane from a statistical footnote of the Rwandan genocide to a man whose suffering is legible. The text's focus on unmasking the terrible transformation and disintegration of the depicted family after the 1994 Rwandan genocide invites readers to imagine what it means to be a man unable to protect and cater for your family because of circumstances beyond your control. Here, perhaps it is instructive to read Kuseremane's almost deranged desire to sing and dance after the death of his mother and the departure of his fiancée as a kind of register. The inter-textual link to Shakespeare's *King Lear* — a fictional character who runs mad rather than make sense or accept his inordinate suffering — is significant because it helps illuminate Kuseremane's action at the close of "Weight of Whispers." Like King Lear before him, Kuseremane runs mad rather than face the intensity of the pain and suffering that has shattered his family. He can express this essence and anguish in a language that is primordial — dance. The dance-cry motif is a register that reminds us of James Berger's argument in another context that trauma is a 'wound that has become a voice' (1997, 577–579). Kuseremane's dance/song mime is a deeply affective register that articulates a reality that is 'in excess of [his] frame of reference' (Felman and Laub 2002, 59).

Conclusion

It is true that Owuor's story opens itself up to multiple readings such as a geopolitical analysis of the significance of the Rwandan genocide on the postcolonial state and security in the Great Lakes Region of Africa. However, it can also benefit from an alternative exploration as my analysis herein suggests. While Kruger, Makokha and Partington read this short story as an exploration of the rupture of the postcolonial subject because of identity politics on which the postcolonial state is anchored, I argue that in many respects this is a text that explores how an individual negotiates the trauma of dislocation and disintegration in trying contexts. Where Partington notes that the significance of Owuor's writing in the East African canon is because her text puts centre stage 'issues of migration and identity [which] were once the playthings of academics [… she] has made them issues of serious importance to us' (2006, 121), one could convincingly counter argue that underneath the themes of identity, migration, postcolonial and state violence lies the theme of individual negotiation of trauma. It is true that the story spotlights the issue of identity and migration because the plot of this text is centred on the Kuseremanes' quest for relocation to the West. However, as my reading suggests, it is plausible to read "Weight of Whispers" as trauma fiction.

This is a point that both Kruger and Partington tangentially make, but unfortunately do not follow-up as they move on to a more important geopolitical reading of the text. For example, Kruger notes that the text is about a 'Tutsi prince escaping from Rwandan genocide [who] laments the loss of his privileged life to the nostalgic tune of "L'Independence cha cha cha' (2009, 1). Similarly, Partington states that the Rwandans who escaped the genocide 'continue to suffer not only the perpetual fear and reality of violence […] but also the rupturing of their desired identities and the impossibility of any stable and peaceful identity' (2006, 118). Both Kruger and Partington are right because across the Great Lakes region many Rwandan refugees such as the Kuseremanes silently mime Kabaselle's tune in acknowledgement of their accursed lives after the genocide. Thus, to a certain extent, it might be valid to read Kuseremane's miming of Kabaselle's hit song as nostalgia for a by-gone era.

Nevertheless, it is also plausible to read Keseremane's miming of Kabaselle's tune as a symbolic expression of the rupture of his mind on account of his suffering. It is further conceivable to argue that because his dancing and singing mimic what Anne Whitehead has elsewhere argued are the 'forms and symptoms' of trauma in their disjointedness, 'repetition and indirection' (2004, 3), the mime becomes a register of scripting his failed quest for a meaningful pattern to his life after escaping Rwanda. I argue that his horrible life is on account of the dangers associated with the postcolonial state. However, when one peels away the layers of African postcolonial political economy, what remains is the bare corporeality of a suffering soul. Read from this perspective, it can be argued that "Weight of Whispers" uses the miming of "L'Independence cha cha cha," the present tense and a diabolically detached and somnambulistic third person and first-person narrative textures to spotlight an individual's disorientation and disintegration in the harsh context of the Great Lakes Region and its ethnic identity politics.

Note

1. The noun 'spouse' in the widow song perhaps accentuates this point. The neutral descriptor can apply to Lune as well as to Kuseremane. When Kuseremane states that Lune was a woman that could have been his wife, it is clear that she is symbolically dead to him. Similarly, when Lune accepts to offer her body in exchange for the visas — whatever justification can be given for this action — she suggests a symbolic erasure (death) of Kuseremane's manhood.

Disclosure Statement

No potential conflict of interest was reported by the author.

References

Adorno, Theodor W. 1983. "Cultural Criticism and Society." In *Prisms*, translated by Samuel and Sherry Weber, 17–34. Cambridge: MIT Press.

Berger James. 1997. "Review: Trauma and Literary Theory. Reviewed Work(s): Unclaimed Experience: Trauma, Narrative and History by Cathy Caruth; Representing the Holocaust: History, Theory, Trauma by Dominick LaCapra; Worlds of Hurt: Reading the Literature of Trauma by Kali Tal." *Contemporary Literature* 38 (3): 569–83. doi:10.2307/1208980.

Berlant, Lauren. 2004. "Introduction: Compassion (and Withholding)." In *Compassion: The Culture and Politics of an Emotion*, edited by Lauren Berlant, 1–4. New York: Routledge.

Douglas, Kate. 2008. "Translating Trauma: Witnessing Bom Bali." *ARIEL: A Review of International English Literature* 39 (1-2): 147–165.

Ekwensi, Cyprian. 1976. *Survive the Peace*. London: Heinemann Educational Books.

Felman, Shoshana, and Dori Laub. 2002. *Testimony: Crises of Witnessing in Literature, Psychoanalysis, and History*. London: Routledge.

Hartman, Geoffrey. 1995. "On Traumatic Knowledge and Literary Studies." *New Literary History* 26 (3): 537–63. doi:10.1353/nlh.1995.0043.

Hartman, Geoffrey. 1998. "Shoah and Intellectual Witness." *Partisan Review (New York, N.Y.)* 65: 37–48.

Kruger, Marie. 2009. "History, Nation, Ghetto: Kenyan Women's Literature on the Ethics of Responsibility." *Postcolonial Text* 5 (3): 1–17.

Makokha, Justus Kizito. 2011. *Ethnic Identities and Gender Themes in Contemporary East African Literature*. PhD dissertation, Freire Universitat, Berlin, Germany.

Nance, Kimberly. 2006. *Can Literature Promote Justice? Trauma, Narrative and Social Actions in Latin American Testimonio.* Nashville: Vanferbilt University Press. doi:10.2307/j.ctv1622n39.

Nussbaum, Martha. 1995. *Poetic Justice: The Literary Imagination and Public Life*. Boston: Beacon Press.

Owuor, Yvonne. 2006. *Weight of Whispers*. Series. Nairobi: Kwani.

Partington, Stephen Derwent. 2006. "Making Us Make Some Sense of Genocide." *Tydeskrif vir Letterunde* 43 (1): 110–21.

Van Alphen, Ernst. 1999. "Symptoms of Discursivity: Experiences, Memory, and Trauma." In *Acts of Memory: Cultural Recall in the Present*, edited by Mieke Bal, Jonathan Crewe, and Leo Spitzer, 24–38. Hanover: University Press of New England.

Whitehead, Anne. 2004. *Trauma Fiction*. Edinburgh: Edinburgh University Press. doi:10.3366/edinburgh/9780748618576.001.0001.

Migrancy as Trauma: Yvonne Owuor's "Weight of Whispers"

Miriam Maranga-Musonye

ABSTRACT
Despite winning the Caine Prize for African Writing in 2003, Yvonne Owuor's "Weight of Whispers" has not received much critical attention. Yet this novella has great potential for understanding Eastern Africa as a cultural and political space as well as the workings of literature in capturing the fragmented realities of the post colony. Thus, I focus on the use of narrative strategies in the novella and how they are used as techniques for narrating trauma; and time and space as two key elements through which the fractured and fragmented nature of character and its subject position within the post colony are presented. I read the fragmentation of the subject in relation to the state's rupture, which in the novella is only alluded to through the mention of the shooting down of the plane carrying the two presidents. I suggest that reading "Weight of Whispers" as a fractured narrative can be productive in understanding key concerns such as migrancy, identity and truth within the context of the trauma narrative.

Introduction

Although Eastern Africa has suffered several cases of mass murders and subsequent emigrations, it was the Rwandese genocide that drew global attention to the region's problem of troubled nationhood. Creative literature continues to capture such crises and the resultant migrations; one such response being Yvonne Owuor's novella, "Weight of Whispers". While much writing on the subject of mass displacement tends to focus more on the collective, ethnic and nationalistic aspects of fractured states, "Weight of Whispers" moves away from these and engages with pain and horror as individualised experiences. It is perhaps with the intention of individualising the pain and trauma that the author declines to name the country the protagonists emigrate from, even though it is possible to infer from a number of details scattered across the story that it is most likely Rwanda.

Postcolonial thinking presents the diffusion resultant from migration, taking place in the context of globalisation, as leading to the blurring of borders and therefore creating new meanings. In view of this, postcolonial critics argue that migrancy has become the name for the condition of human beings in the twenty-first century. Commenting on postcolonial discourses on migrancy, Andrew Smith (2004b) observes that discussions of migrancy or of the figure of the exile are almost always discussions of the subject who has left a birthplace elsewhere for residence and work in Europe, North America, or Australia (63). This general trend raises the question of the nature of exile in the context of violent upheavals especially within Africa, which is the situation presented in "Weight of Whispers". Within the broad postcolonial discourse on migrancy, this essay focuses on *identity, truth* and *agency* from the perspective of *trauma* and seeks to present an analysis of "Weight of Whispers" as a seminal rendition of trauma and its impact on the individual who is spatio-temporally removed from the sites of the traumatising events.

The question of *identity* within migrancy is captured in Stuart Hall's (2013) argument on homelessness in his assertion that 'what was initially felt to be a curse ... — the curse of homelessness or the curse of enforced exile — gets repossessed as a privileged standpoint from which certain useful and critical perceptions about the modern world become more likely. Postcolonial discourse celebrates migrancy as the space in which the condition and identity of transnational subjects is located since by becoming mobile and making narratives out of their mobility, people escape the control of states and national borders and the limited linear ways of understanding themselves. In the words of Lazarus (2004), 'If human beings have tended to understand themselves as citizens of nations or as blood members of ethnic groupings, migration increasingly exposes the insufficiency of these ways of identifying ourselves' (249). The postcolonial idea that there are no longer any set centres, definite horizons or clear limits since humans now live in an in-between-space, is underscored in Homi Bhabha's (1994) assertion that there is no necessary or eternal belongingness (179); therefore, one's identity is not eternally tied to a specific place of origin, essential culture or lineage, but its new essence is in the migrant's state of mobility and fluidity.

Related to the idea of new identities resulting from cultural transgressions and transnational flows, is the question of the relativity of *truth* as expressed through the postcolonial fascination with subjectivities embodied in migrancy. Within postcolonial discourse, history itself is a contested sphere as pointed out by Hayden White (1987) in his argument that official history is told from a particular social centre which neglects other histories and is consequently subjective (11). Andrew Smith observes that postcolonial perceptions of migrancy are characterised by 'a sense of cultural relativity, a constructivist wariness over any claims to truth or to certain knowledge, and an assertion of the centrality of the imagination or fantasy in social organization' (2004b, 63). This implies that migrancy gives impetus to the subject to create new perspectives and to free the self from the restrictions of master narratives and official history.

Postcolonial thinking presents migrancy as an experience which engenders new opportunities and possibilities therefore conferring *agency* to the migrant. The ideas of Homi Bhabha are foundational in the postcolonial perception of migrancy as a space of meaning and agency. Bhabha argues that there is no inherent purity of cultures; therefore, it is the in-between space of cultural interaction that carries the burden of cultural meaning. He further argues that cultures transgress and transform each other in complex ways, leading to new perceptions and meanings (1985, 1994). Along the same line, Salman Rushdie (1991) proposes that in postcolonial reality, the outdated idea of nostalgia for a homeland as a specific place is replaced with the creative power of the imagination. In these arguments, it is implied that through the creative power of the imagination, the migrant subject gains agency.

Whereas the above notions present migrancy as conveying a productive sense of identity, truth and agency, the reality presented in "Weight of Whispers" raises questions regarding the productivity of migrancy as a general condition. Consequently, I focus on the characters' sense of identity, truth and agency in the context of the confounding realities of forced exile and argue that they can only be productively apprehended by focusing on them from a perspective of trauma. The essay presents the trauma approach as a productive way of understanding postcolonial tribulations. If it true as Cathy Caruth (1995) argues that the traumatised carry an impossible history within them, or become themselves the symptoms of a history they cannot entirely possess, then a productive reading of migrant subjects such as the Kuseremanes needs to take into consideration the effect of the harrowing experience of the atrocities witnessed or committed and recognise trauma as defining their sense of identity, truth and agency.

Migrancy and the Crisis of Identity

In "Weight of Whispers", we see two types of migrancies: the first is represented by Boniface's season of European sojourn when he worked as a diplomat and as a gems dealer, while the second is represented by his and his family's flight to Kenya and their thwarted attempt to go to Europe. These two seasons are used to interrogate the notion of the privileged position of migrancy especially in the context of the aftermath of traumatic experiences in fractured post-colonial states.

Three aspects associated with the concept of identity are being, self-awareness and belonging. Traditionally, one's identity revolves around a sense of conscious knowledge of one's existence and rootedness within certain parameters including family, clan, nation and class among others. For the most part, people are not overly concerned with the question of self-identity and therefore these elements are taken for granted. As Anthony Kerby (1991) puts it, 'Questions of identity and self-understanding arise primarily in crisis situations and at certain turning points in our routine behaviour' (6). Postcolonial discourse presents migrancy as a site where a pre-constituted identity is challenged and new identities forged within the in-between space of cultural subjectivity engendered by exile. One of the key tenets of postcolonial discourse is that identity is deterritorialised. Stuart Hall (2013) argues that the idea of essential unity based on blood and land are at best fictions that people put to work to think of themselves as a single congregation.

In "Weight of Whispers", the question of identity is quite enigmatic. The author refrains from giving the reader a clear indication of the identity of the narrator and other key characters. The reader must glean the story from snatches of exposition and dramatisation which point to the identity of characters. In the beginning section of the plot, the narrator introduces himself and his family directly, but still without revealing much about their background: 'I am Boniface Louis R. Kuseremane. … The "R" stands for a name that cannot be spoken aloud. … I glance at Agnethe-mama, regal, graying; her diamond earrings dance, her nose held high, her forehead unlined … ' (Owuor 2006, 13).

Through the Kuseremanes experience as exiles in Nairobi, the identity anchors they have so far taken for granted are contested and presented as untenable. The unravelling of their identity markers of nationality, royalty, ethnicity and socio-economic status fits neatly within postcolonial discourse which argues that such identity markers are rendered insufficient by the realities of migration. The unravelling of identity anchors for the Kuseremanes is captured succinctly in the narrator's words when he refers to himself as a man who *used to be a prince in a land eviscerated*, which points to the disembowelling of two key identity markers: his royal heritage and his nationality. His identity is tied to his royalty, nationality and human dignity and their loss forces upon him the necessity to reconfigure a new identity within his current situation of exile.

Homi Bhabha's argument that there is no necessary or eternal belongingness since humans now live in an in-between-space (1994, 179) would imply that transnational subjects such as the Kuseremanes should be at home anywhere in the world. The postcolonial idea that through mobility people escape the control of states and broaden their ways of understanding themselves is demonstrated through Boniface's season of European sojourn, during which his mobility across different parts of the world, especially Europe, was significant in defining him as a global citizen. At the time, he took his mobility for granted and could even afford to dislike certain European cities such as London. Now, he is in a season of another type of mobility; he has left his country and is in Kenya enroute to Europe, but he finds himself trapped in this in-between space which he had hoped was a mere stop-over.

Despite Boniface's protestations that he is an international citizen, the reality is that at this time he and his family belong to a borderline community of forced immigrants. In the Kuseremanes' derelict life in the margins of Nairobi city, we see no repossession and transformation of the curse of homelessness. Instead, through Boniface, we see the presentation of the figure of the exile as one displaced not just from mainstream society but also from the realm of what is considered normal and moral. The trauma he has experienced pushes him to the fringes of normalcy and morality. His friends and country people do not trust him, partly because of his perceived role in the genocide and partly because they think he is a financial and moral burden. Through the indeterminate issue of Boniface's participation in the genocide, Owuor invites us to question moral identities through the implicit question of whether Boniface is as evil as his countrymen perceive him to be or, conversely, whether he is as innocent as he presents himself to be.

At the heart of this underlying moral question is the rupture and pathology caused by traumatic experience. Boniface is presented not just as a political fugitive, but essentially as a moral fugitive; one who is pursued by 'whispers' and phantoms from his past which is the essence of his traumatised psyche. Cathy Caruth's (1995) assertion that 'to be traumatized is simply to be possessed by an image or event' (4–5) appears quite true of Boniface whose present is completely consumed by his past experiences and/or actions, leading to a crisis of identity. Caruth's further assertion that trauma causes radical disruptions and gaps because it brings us to the limits of our understanding (4) can help in understanding the crisis of identity that Boniface and his family experience as marginal characters in exile. Owuor narrates this crisis of identity or 'curse' of exile by manipulating the setting in "Weight of Whispers" in a manner that creates gaps and disruptions in the protagonist's psyche.

The disruptions and gaps are captured through the use of minimal description of setting and erratic shifts in setting. On the whole, setting in the novella is not described in any concrete sense. We are given names of streets such as Kenyatta Avenue, Kaunda Street, River Road; places such as The Hilton, the American Embassy, UNHCR offices and Club Balafon but not much else besides. The minimal description conveys the sense of lostness experienced by the protagonist and his family. This lostness is aggravated by their linguistic alienation as French speakers in an Anglophone country, which the protagonist calls a 'sea of English' (Owuor 2006, 15).

Minimal description also indicates the migrant's preoccupation with matters of basic survival; for example, after the narrator is thrown out of a jewellery shop by the Indian lady proprietor, he walks out into the street and is dazed by the pain of being conned and humiliated. In this state, his mind cannot register anything about his physical environment, which is captured through the minimal description which helps to underscore his desperate state as an exile. The Rwandan Embassy in Nairobi is simply referred to as 'gates ... locked and barred' (Owuor 2006, 15). In the narrator's situation and state of mind, it seems there is not much that he can register about the embassy except signs that send a clear message to him about his plight, in this case, the locked and barred gates.

While the embassy should be a home away from home, it has now turned into a signifier for the absence of a home.

"Weight of Whispers" is also characterised by liberal shifts in setting, moving the reader from one location to the next without any transition. Setting in the narrative is used not so much as a concrete location, but as a space for action in which the migrant subject tries to rediscover himself. This style indicates that the protagonist is postponing reflection over painful experiences and secondly indicates his attempt to maintain his sanity by simply walking from place to place.

When Boniface goes to seek a work permit at the immigration office, there is a sudden shift to a different scene at the point when the reader expects a narration of what happens at the office. Immediately the immigration officer calls out 'next' for Boniface to be served, the scene instantaneously shifts to a travel agency on Kaunda Street. Then again it immediately shifts to a church building in the city where he is sitting at the porch. Only then, as he sits and watches the lunchtime worshippers, does he allow himself to think about the humiliation he was subjected to by the immigration officer's scathing comment, *'Ati PhD? PhD gani? Wewe refugee, bwana'* (Owuor 2006, 33). [PhD? What PhD? You are a refugee, man].

Though often taken for granted, a name is a basic marker of identity. While in exile in Nairobi, Boniface comes face to face with the total implication of a name to one's identity. We get a hint quite early in the story that his name is a negative identification marker when he says that the 'R' in his name stands for a name that cannot be spoken aloud. While he begins by hiding only one name, the debilitating experience of exile, coupled with a haunting past, push him to the point where he has to hide all his names. At the immigration office he gives his name as Rene Katilibana; when he is arrested and asked his name by the police officer, he cannot bring himself to utter it. In his mind he asks, 'What is my name?' Stephen Partington (1989) refers to Boniface's inability to utter his own name in public as a symbolic act of self-abnegation (6) which is referred to in the narrative as psychic oblation.

The obliteration of a name as a key identity marker is emphasised by the role played by the global mobility regime and the local authorities in Kenya which relegate the narrator and his family to the margins. Boniface spends a lot of time in queues where he constantly hears the word 'Next' shouted to him from across counters. This word emphasises his powerlessness and makes him feel depersonalised. His situation as a forced migrant has reduced him from a human being to just another item in a queue.

Although globalisation is generally seen to lead to the blurring and dissolving of international boundaries (Sackeyfio 2014, 199), the reality for the post-violence migrant is that the global mobility regime continues to erect more barriers in the form of stringent requirements for residency, mobility and resettlement, thus reducing the post-violence migrant to a beggar. In Nairobi, the Kuseremanes belong to a marginal community of refugees who are a small minority in terms of demographics; yet, they are looked at with suspicion despite their marginality and minority.

Arjun Appadurai (2006) explains the irony implied in the fear the majority have towards minorities by focusing on the tension between the perceived totality and completeness of the majority, on the one hand, and the disruption caused by the minority, on the other. He argues that '... it is precisely the smallness of the gap between national totality and minority presence that produces the anxiety of incompleteness and creates the frustration and rage that drives those forms of degradation that shock us...' (56–57). This would explain the scathing comment by the immigration officer to Boniface, *PhD? What PhD? You are a refugee, man!*. It is driven by the immigration officer's fear of what he perceives Boniface to represent — a threat to national completeness and wholeness. The subtext in the comment is that being a refugee, Kusereman does not belong and therefore has no right to claim any legitimacy despite his high level of education.

Migrancy and the Crisis of Truth

Creative literature — whether historical or not — exists against the background of experiential history which it is expected to illuminate. The postcolonial idea that history itself is a contested sphere implies that the relationship between creative literature and fictional characters, on the one hand, and history on the other, is always already problematic. This gives creative literature the power to challenge official historical discourses and present other histories. Subjectivity is therefore celebrated as a site of productivity through imagination and new perspectives, but when we consider migrancy resulting from political violence in fractured states, the positive image of subjectivity and relativity begins to unravel. What is dramatised in "Weight of Whispers" demonstrates that forced migration thrusts the migrant into a crisis of truth both at the personal and the national level. Due to the precarious position of the Kuseremanes, they try to reconstruct a certain truth around their lives, but this constructed personal and national truth remains indeterminate throughout the narrative. Boniface constantly uses physical appearance to describe himself and his family members. He constantly refers to himself as a very tall man; and his three female family members as elegant and bejewelled, which is a pointer to their regal appearance and royal status. Significantly, Owuor declines to give the ethnic identity of the protagonist and his family although their physical description and royal heritage would lead to the conclusion that they are Tutsi, but this is left indeterminate. The possibility that the protagonist family is from the Tutsi community of course raises the question how come they would have been involved in the genocide, yet historically, it is the Hutu who were the key perpetrators.

Through narrative indeterminacy, Owuor demonstrates how migrancy causes a crisis of truth whereby migrants are forced to filter the truth because their survival may very well depend on what is known about their background, history and identity. Memory and history thus become tools to be manipulated. If the notion advocated by Anthony Kerby (1991) about the relationship between memory and identity is taken into consideration, then the working of Boniface's memory within the context of migrancy becomes more complex. Kerby argues that memory is closely related to personal identity because people define themselves in terms of the lived experiences of their lives (Kerby 1991, 21). Boniface's past, coupled with his precarious position as a migrant in Kenya leads to altering or even total obliteration of some of his lived experiences. This altering and obliteration are pointers to the complex nature of understanding truth in the context of trauma as implied by Caruth's (1995) argument that the traumatised carry an impossible history within them, or they become themselves the symptoms of a history they cannot entirely possess (5).

At the level of narrative, this is done through the use of ellipsis as a narrative strategy. The elimination of such elements creates gaps whose degree of visibility depends on what the protagonist wishes to accomplish using the ellipses. As a narrative strategy, ellipsis works through indirection to emphasise by understatement or non-statement. The elliptical gaps create fractures in the narrative causing it to be indeterminate, especially if the elided details are not confirmed within the particular narrative itself. Consequently, ellipsis becomes a productive narrative trope for presenting and investigating the question of truth.

Commenting on ellipsis, Mieke Bal (1997) observes that in narrative, an event about which nothing is said may have been so painful that it is preferable to maintain complete silence about it (71). This is further complicated, as Okaka Dokotum (2014) points out, by the difficulty of narrating traumatic experiences due to the susceptibility of history to disjointed memory reconstruction which is affected by the fact that the victim-witnesses may still be in the process of coming to terms with the violence (9).

"Weight of Whispers" is mainly presented through stream of consciousness, a style which renders itself easily to use of ellipsis because it is characterised by disjointed and sometimes unconnected thought processes. A key ellipsis in the story is the lack of mention of the country of origin of the Kuseremane family. The anchoring statement which enables the reader to situate the story historically and geographically is made in one sentence, 'Two presidents died when a missile launched from the ground brought their plane down' (Owuor 2006, 7). This is a reference to the 1994 killing of Juvenal Habyarimana, the president of Rwanda, and his Burundian counterpart, an event that is largely seen to have been a major catalyst of the genocide which took place in Rwanda soon after. In this one sentence summary, which provides the historical background and context of the unfolding events, neither the words Rwanda and genocide nor the names of the presidents nor even the names of the major communities involved in the genocide are mentioned. This basic ellipsis invites the reader to interpret the contextual truth and history.

A key aspect of the truth about the Kuseremanes' identity as victims or culprits in the genocide has to do with the time when they left their country for Nairobi. Boniface says that they left on the fifth day after the killing of the presidents. The first time he says it, there seems to be no doubt and it comes across as a statement of simple fact: 'He [Roger, their servant] reappeared at our door on the evening of the fifth day after the death of the two presidents' (Owuor 2006, 11). The narrator says that they boarded the last flight out of the city on the day of Roger's bizarre reappearance and his announcement of an impending counterattack with the words, 'They are coming ... Sir' (Owuor 2006, 12). Later, however, after he learns that his name is likely to be on the list of genocidaires, he refers to the timing of their departure in a manner that indicates that it is a contested issue and therefore has to be asserted emphatically, almost as if he is trying to convince himself, 'But we had left on the fifth day!' (Owuor 2006, 28). The third and final time he refers to their departure, it is in the form of a question, which clearly casts doubt on the matter, 'But hadn't we left on the fifth day?' (Owuor 2006, 55). The specificity of the timing of their departure is crucial in determining whether he participated in the genocide or not. The question that is left in the reader's mind is whether the narrator has actually forgotten the particular date of their departure or is deliberately mixing it up. As Kerby (1991) observes, recollection like perception involves a considerable degree of interpretation since the past is rarely, if ever, unfolded in the same way twice (31). While the interpretation of the past is characteristic of human experience, it acquires a special edge within the context of migrancy, especially forced migration, because of the need for migrants to position themselves anew in the new world into which they is thrust.

"Weight of Whispers" raises many questions about narrative truth and historical truth. Since it is told by a first-person narrator, it could be taken as authentic and believable because the teller is a participant. Conversely, it could be seen as mendacious because the narrator is the only one who tells and there is little in the narrative against which to countercheck the truth of what he tells. The unreliability of Boniface as a narrator has been pointed out by various critics, including Justus Makokha (2011) and Partington (2006). Makokha argues that having the protagonist as a first-person narrator, who also has symptoms of psychological instability, makes Boniface an unreliable narrator. He points out too that the narrator seems to make a deliberate attempt to deceive the audience, and this underscores his unreliability (96). Partington (2006) goes a step further to make the claim that Boniface is not only unreliable as a narrator but is massively fragmented — in fact a cancelled character: '[a] textual construct of the type that [Boniface] Kuseremane clearly is, and one that at no time has a coherent identity/subject platform from which to speak, is not only unreliable, it is impossible

— it is a narrator that not only cannot understand itself, but that also cannot possibly articulate itself' (15).

While postcolonial studies privilege the migrant as one who is in a position to see more clearly due to his/her unique position as an insider-outsider, the position of Boniface in "Weight of Whispers" seems to challenge this view. Caught in the throes of trying to survive in a foreign land, his insights are tainted by the lack of agency occasioned by the debilitating conditions of exile. Despite this, Boniface's unreliability as a narrator is one of the techniques used by Owuor to create a story with great possibilities for meaning, making it productive in dealing with a complex subject such as the effects of forced migration. The author's deliberately elliptical style and tentativeness underscore the view that she seems to be inviting the reader to actively engage not just with the text, but with the extratextual realities that inform the text, including political instability, failed leadership and ethnicity among other post-colonial realities, but most significantly, an engagement with trauma as a singular and individualised experience.

Whether Boniface is unable or unwilling to tell the truth, his position as a migrant subject indicates his precarious position as an escapee of violence and his troubled psyche due to trauma. He confesses to having dreams in which blood flows out of phantom mouths, which in itself indicates an encounter or experience of a violent event; yet, he does not seem to possess any conscious knowledge of this violence. A focus on the nature of trauma can help us understand this paradox. Caruth (1995) argues that the dreams and hallucinations people experience in the aftermath of harrowing experiences are not *possessed* by the traumatised as knowledge, but on the contrary, they *possess* the victim as trauma and so, paradoxically, for this reason, instead of the dreams and hallucinations confirming the truth and reality of the traumatic experience, they cause a deep uncertainty about it (6). This might explain why Boniface seems to gloss over the recent historical happenings which have brought him to his current position. At the level of the narrative, this is done by use of summary, the presentation of events in a sketchy fast pace. This strategy is usually used to tell 'insignificant' events which do not influence the course of the narrative such as daily routines (Bal 1997, 71). Summaries occur often enough in narrative fiction because they help the writer to quickly transition to the next significant scene. However, when a very significant event in a narrative is presented in the form of summary, attention is drawn to it because of the discrepancy between what the reader expects and what is offered. In "Weight of Whispers" summary is used as a form of euphemistic strategy through which serious subjects are seemingly minimised or diverted.

Throughout the whole story the only direct reference to the genocide is given in a one paragraph summary:

> We had heard rumours of a holocaust, of a land hemorrhaging to death. Everywhere hoarse murmurs, eyes white and wide with an arcane fear. Is it possible that brothers

> would machete sisters-in law to stew-meat size chunks in front of nephews and nieces? (Owuor 2006, 8)

Significantly, the author does not return to this issue to confirm if it was true or simply rumours; the matter is left indeterminate. The summarising of the details of an event of such enormity as the genocide draws attention to the nature of the narrating protagonist. It would seem that the narrator is trying to distance himself from the violence and horror by failing to confirm whether the events actually took place or not. And yet as a result of those 'rumours' the narrator and his family flee their home country and come to seek refuge in Nairobi, for a few days as they organise to move to Europe.

The author's unconventional use of summary becomes a silence on the part of the narrating protagonist. Throughout the narrative, the narrator maintains a telling vagueness and subjectivity concerning his involvement in the genocide and consequently how his name may have found its way onto the list of genocidaires. At the level of interpretation, the reader is prompted to ask why the narrator only sketchily makes reference to the genocide — its genesis, execution and aftermath. Perhaps, as we have seen earlier, he is postponing the confrontation to another time; yet, the narrative ends without him directly confronting it. Another interpretation we can give it is that he is afraid to even think about it as if thinking about it will make its effects catch up with him. Or simply that due to the trauma, he no longer possesses these experiences and events in his mind as conscious knowledge or truth or as lived history.

In postcolonial discourse subjectivity is presented as a site of possibilities, freeing the migrant from constricting social norms. While in postcolonial discourse the mutability and contestability of history, cultural values and facts is offered as desirable due to its ability to confer power and agency, the reality of migrancy in the aftermath of gross political violence as seen in "Weight of Whispers" shows that rather than convey agency and power, the mutability embodies a crisis of truth that may be a means of hiding complicity or culpability.

Migrancy and the Crisis of Agency

Postcolonial postulations about migrancy imply that transnational subjects such as the Kuseremanes should be at home anywhere in the world. Yet, although the protagonist and the other migrant characters in "Weight of Whispers" hardly ever say it directly, it is clear that they are traumatised by the experience of displacement. The onslaught on human dignity engendered by exile results in tensions between migrancy and agency leading to a troubled psyche and arrested agency which Owuor presents through the narrative strategy of anachrony, presented either as retroversion or anticipation.

The story begins with a humiliating and dehumanising encounter between Boniface and a policeman in a cell during which the policeman steals all valuables from Boniface and slaps him hard on the face. This incident takes place several months after the arrival of the narrator and his family in Nairobi. It is only later that we are given the details of their flight from their country and arrival in Nairobi. By choosing this incident as the plot's beginning, Owuor immerses the reader deep into the quagmire of life for a refugee in Nairobi. In a case of anachronic anticipation, the narrator reacts to the slap by making the following mental note: 'Later, much later on, I will wonder what makes it possible for one man to hit another … But now, I lower my head. The sum total of what resides in a very tall man who used to be a prince in a land eviscerated' (Owuor 2006, 7). He has been subjected to psychological and physical abuse and he feels bitter towards the policeman whom he sees as both physically disgusting and morally corrupt. Yet, despite the fact that as readers we can see his humiliation, he refuses to acknowledge it; instead, he postpones this to a future time. This postponement is an indication that he is traumatised and deprived of agency.

The story moves back and forth in time and in most cases without any transition statements. One key instance of retroversion or moving back in time is seen where Boniface tells about his experiences during the season of his European sojourn (Owuor 2006, 8–10). This information interrupts the present of the narrative and is used to emphasise his plight by showing the contrast between the life he lived as a diplomat and his present life as a forced migrant. He remembers that during that time he came across people experiencing residual trauma and trying to obliterate a painful past or to raise a memorial to a perceived injustice from the past. In each of these cases, the individuals still exhibit strong emotions such as pain, bitterness or denial. At the time, these pathological reactions did not make sense to him, and he could afford to walk away from it all or play with words or even be amused.

In the present, the situation is different as we see in the sentence which marks the end of this retroversion, 'Now my world has tilted into a realm where other loaded silences lurk' (Owuor 2006, 10). He is now in the second type of migrancy which is a far cry from the international travels of his earlier self. Like the pathological subjects mentioned in the retroversion, he too is trying to exorcise the daemons of his past by 'turning away'. He reflects that 'In the empire of silence the act of "turning away" is a vain exorcism of a familiar daemon that breaches the citadels we ever change, ever fortify again. Dragging us back through old routes of anguish, it suggests: "Alas, human, your nature relishes fratricidal blood."' (Owuor 2006, 10). Within "Weight of Whispers", the troubled psyche of the postcolonial, post-violence migrant, the metaphorical 'empire of silence' is rendered through the liberal use of ellipsis as a narrative strategy. The desperate situation of the migrant subject is seen in that the exorcism through silence and turning away is a futile exercise for Boniface as he is always constantly dragged back into the anguish of his past; this kind of *possession* is the essence of trauma.

Sigmund Freud's foundational ideas about human response to trauma are applicable here. According to Freud, the mind goes into shock, upon experiencing violence and the full impact of the violence is not known to the victim at the time of the experience but returns later as dreams and nightmares (Plotnik 1989, 413). Ron Singer (2007) makes the observation that "Weight of Whispers" captures the nightmare of African dislocation through an array of technical elements including the description of the terrors of being chased and run to ground by demons from one's own past (Singer, 5–6). Boniface alludes to these demons from the past when he observes that '... some things must remain buried in silence, even if they resurrect themselves at night in dreams in which blood pours out of phantom mouths' (Owuor 2006, 10). The reality of the horror of traumatic experiences implied in "Weight of Whispers" is made more poignant if looked at through the lens of Caruth's (1995) assertion that traumatic dreams, hallucinations and flashbacks are not symbolic, but literal in an unexplainable way since they constantly take the traumatised back to the traumatising event and in this way remain true to the event (5).

The embedding of these incidences from the protagonist's past at this particular point in the plot, highlights his decline from a global diplomat to a destitute, roaming the streets of Nairobi. More importantly, it shows his transition from voice to silence. During the season of his European sojourn, he had opinions and questions for almost every situation; now he has entered the empire of silence due to the realisation that any seemingly harmless question or comment is potentially explosive. In most cases silence is not a conscious choice on his part, but a condition he is forced into by his present circumstances. While postcolonial critics such as Salman Rushdie (1991) emphasise that the power of the creative imagination replaces the nostalgia for a spatial homeland, in the case of Boniface, it would seem that the absence of nostalgia for his homeland leaves only a void as he is homeless and voiceless and therefore without agency.

Boniface's failure to tell a lot of the events which the reader naturally assumes or knows to have taken place may be read as an attempt to expunge these experiences from his consciousness or even obliterate them from history. He uses silence as a form of exorcism of negative experiences as a coping mechanism in dealing with trauma, but also as a means of re-constructing truth for survival.

The loss of agency for the migrant is also dramatised through shifting perspectives whereby the story which is mainly in the first person shifts to the third person at specific moments. Some critics have interpreted this style as a way of indicating the narrator's attempt to hide his complicity in the genocide. Makokha (2011), for instance, argues that as a general rule, Boniface escapes to the third person perspective when talking about the egregious things that he is unwilling to admit to have done. Further to this, one may argue that each time the narrator shifts from the first to third person perspective, it is with the intention of hiding from the reality of the pain of an experience or a memory. This escape demonstrates a crisis of agency since he is unable to act in any meaningful way to change his situation and that of his family; for example, when he assaults his sister, he says, 'I frown when I see the tall dark man lift his hand up, right up and bring it crashing down on the back of the girl who collapses to the floor, lies flat on her belly and stops crying … ' (Owuor 2006, 60). Although Boniface does not acknowledge it directly, it is clear that this physical assault is what triggers Chi-Chi's miscarriage which takes place a few hours later and quickly leads to her death. At her deathbed the hint of the connection between the assault and the miscarriage is given through Boniface's words, again presented in the third person, 'I remember a blow delivered on her defenseless back by a defenseless brother-prince' (Owuor 2006, 62).

In "Weight of Whispers" we observe not only the crisis of agency undermining the migrants, but also the demands of survival ravaging their physical bodies; the two processes lead to the disintegration of their emotional beings and the ravaging of their physical bodies. Although Lune and Boniface escape physical death, the narrative leaves no doubt that the ravages of exile have etched their souls in a manner from which they are unlikely to recover. The Kuseremanes' unfolding drama points to the questioning of key postcolonial ideas on migrancy under the special circumstances of forced displacement, for example Bhabha's argument that the in-between space of cultural interaction is what produces new perceptions and meanings (1985, 1994). While in-betweenness and hybridity are realities whose productivity cannot be denied, a dispassionate look at the in-betweenness resulting from violent forced displacement as in the case of the Kuseremanes, seems to strongly suggest that migrancy should not be over-generalised and romanticised. One may argue that the protagonist does gain some critical perceptions about himself and the world, but only at the expense of his own self.

The ravages of exile have eliminated for the narrator the option of resettlement in a third country. Having buried his sister and mother in Kenyan soil, it seems that he is unable to leave and start life afresh. As Lune is soaring the skies headed for Canada, he sits on top of his mother's grave, gripped by a new level of awareness that only the stripping experience of exile could engender. He now understands life to be a voyeur possessed of an inexorable power to extinguish itself; and with this new consciousness, all his strivings to control the vagaries of life are stilled. This new awareness ironically underscores his squashed agency.

Conclusion

At the beginning, I observed that the discussion of migrancy or of the figure of the exile in literature is almost always a discussion of the subject who has left a birthplace elsewhere for residence and work in Europe, North America, or Australia. It would seem that the celebrated migrant is the intellectual, adventurer or businessperson who is able to move freely from one continent to the other and take advantage of the space availed by migrancy to forge new identities as a world citizen. Under such circumstances, the migrant subject may not need to rely on nationhood, blood ties or ethnic groupings as identity anchors, which presents migrancy as a metaphor for the nature of human existence in the twenty-first century and beyond. Such migrant subjects may afford to replace the 'outdated' idea of nostalgia for a homeland as a specific place with the creative power of the imagination as advocated by Salman Rushdie (1991). Yet, as demonstrated through the analysis of the Kuseremanes' experience as exiles in Kenya, migrancy as an experience is not homogenous and it is not always a site of desirable new possibilities.

Boniface confesses that he and his family have an affinity for Europe and perhaps as a consequence of this, they seem not able to spare any tangible positive thought for their eviscerated country. There seems to be a danger in the privileging of migrancy as the site of new identity and sense of being not only because of the possibility of justifying African elites' apathy towards the African predicament, but also glossing over the traumatic effects than migrancy can have on the individual psyche.

Partington (2006) argues that the tragedy suffered by the Kuseremanes highlights the downside of the postmodern-postcolonial 'cult of the migrant' which presents nomadism and migration as examples of the most productive forms of cultural identity. According to him, this can only work in the case of former colonial subjects who are now comfortable in privileged, wealthy western universities in peaceful countries (13–14).

In postcolonial thinking, the migrant is seen to be in a position of peculiar insight because he/she has the specific awareness of the relativity of cultural rules and norms. It cannot be denied that the Kuseremanes gain a lot of insight from their experience as exiles in Nairobi; yet, this insight does not convey agency on them as migrant subjects. Instead, it seems to lead to the erasure of identity and agency as signified by Boniface's inability to utter his own name in public and his final confession that he has joined the sentinels of the cemetery as he waits for the return of a name set ablaze when fire made dust out of two presidents' bodies … (Owuor 2006, 69).

Disclosure Statement

No potential conflict of interest was reported by the author.

References

Appadurai, Arjun. 2006. *Fear of Small Numbers: An Essay on the Geography of Anger*. Durham, London: Duke University Press.

Bal, Mieke. 1997. *Narratology: Introduction to the Theory of Narrative*. Toronto: University of Toronto Press.

Bhabha, Homi. 1985. "Signs Taken for Wonders: Questions of Ambivalence and Authority under a Tree Outside Delhi, May1817." *Critical Inquiry* 12 (1): 144–165.

Bhabha, Homi. 1994. *The Location of Culture*. London: Routledge.

Caruth, Cathy, ed. 1995. *Trauma: Explorations in Meaning*. London: Johns Hopkins University Press.

Dokotum, Okaka Opio. 2014. "Trauma Aesthetics in War Documentaries about the Lord's Resistance Army in Uganda." *Eastern African Literary and Cultural Studies* 1 (1-2): 7–16. doi:10.1080/23277408.2014.941749.

Hall, Stuart. 2003. "Cultural Identity and Diaspora". In *Colonial Discourse and Postcolonial Theory. A Reader*, edited by Patrick Williams and Laura Chrisman, 392–403. London & New York: Routledge – Taylor & Francis Group.

Kerby, Anthony Paul. 1991. *Narrative and the Self.* Bloomington, Indianapolis: Indiana University Press.

Lazarus, Neil, ed. 2004. *Postcolonial Literary Studies*. Cambridge: Cambridge University Press. doi:10.1017/CCOL0521826942.

Makokha, Justus Kizito. 2011. *Ethnic Identities and Gender Themes in Contemporary East African Literature*. Dissertation. Berlin: Free University of Berlin. http://www.diss.fu-berlin.de/diss/servlets/MCRFileNodeServlet/FUDISS_derivate_000000009814/MAKOKHA_DISSERTATION.pdf.

Owuor, Yvonne Adhiambo. 2006. *"Weight of Whispers."* Nairobi: Kwani Trust.

Partington, Stephen Derwent. 2006. "Making us Make some Sense of Genocide: Beyond the cancelled character of Kuseremane in Yvonne Adhiambo Owuor's 'Weight of Whispers'." *Tydskrif vir Letterkunde* 43 (1). doi:10.4314/tvl.v43i1.29721.

Plotnik, Rod. 1989. *Introduction to Psychology*. 2nd ed. New York. Random House.

Rushdie, Salman. 1991. *Imaginary Homelands: Essays in Criticism 1981*–1991. London: Granta.

Sackeyfio, Rose A. 2014. "Black Women's Bodies in a Global Economy: Sex, Lies and Slavery in *Trafficked* and *On Black Sister Street*." In *At the Crossroads: Readings of the Postcolonial and the Global in African Literature and Visual Art*, edited by Ghirmai Negash, Andrea Frohne, and Samuel Zadi, 199–210. Trenton: African World Press.

Singer, Ron 2007. *"Un Cri de Coeur from Africa to the World: Yvette [sic] Adhiambo Owuor s 'Weight of Whispers'." The Georgia Review* 61 (2): 401–421. http://www.jstor.org/stable/41402861.

Smith, Andrew. 2004a. "Migrancy, Hybridity and Postcolonial Literary Studies." In *Postcolonial Literary Studies*, edited by Neil Lazarus, 241–260. Cambridge: Cambridge University Press. doi:10.1017/CCOL0521826942.013.

Smith, Andrew. 2004b. "Reading against the Postcolonial Grain: Migrancy and Exile in the Short Stories of Kanchana Ugbabe." *Research in African Literatures* 35 (3): 62–75. http://www.jstor.org/stable/3821294.

White, Hayden. 1987. *The Content of Form: Narrative Discourse and Historical Representation*. Baltimore, Md.: Johns Hopkins University Press.

Rhizomic Writing and Reading of a Nation Coming to Birth in Yvonne A. Owuor's Novel, *Dust*

Christopher Odhiambo Joseph

ABSTRACT
Anchored on Deleueze and Guattari's notion of rhizome, this article inspects the narrative strategy in Yvonne Owuor's novel, *Dust*, in imagining the Kenyan nation, especially in the context of the contested presidential elections of 2007. It subsequently grapples with how Owuor weaves and patches different instances and moments of remembering into connected rhizomic-like narratives, coalescing into the vision of a nation; fragmented, but hankering for forgiveness, healing and a wrestling with a sense of coming to birth and nationhood. From a rhizomic reading of the novel, the article scrutinises how the private and public remembering intersects and inter-texts with fiction and real lived experiences (history) in narrating the evinced vision of the coming to birth of the post-independence Kenyan nation.

Introduction

Yvonne A. Owuor's novel *Dust* seems to follow the path of literary imaginaries that deploy death to explore subjugated histories of the marginalised, discriminated and oppressed communities and to register experiences and history of a nation grappling with complexities of coming to birth. This is consistent with literary imaginaries such as Richard Wright's (1940) novel *Native Son*, Dennis Scott's (1986) play *An Echo in the Bone* and Francis Imbuga's (1976) play *Betrayal in the City*, all which in varying degrees of complexity, employ death and dead bodies to generate narratives about nations. In Wright's *Native Son*, for instance, Bigger Thomas' killing of a white rich young woman is wittingly deployed to interrogate the real meaning of the American dream in relation to the African-American. This act of murder, as well as subsequent actions of Bigger Thomas, cannot be interpreted and fully understood without a backward glance into the history of the American nation and society. Dennis Scott's play *An Echo in the Bone* follows a similar trajectory where an act of murder becomes central in understanding a history of racial relationships in the West Indies, while in Francis Imbuga's play,

Betrayal in the City, the death of Adika, a university student, is deployed as a dramatic organising structure to demonstrate the ironies of the emerging post-independent Kenyan nation.

Owuor similarly utilises death as a framing and structuring trope in *Dust* in interpreting and laying bare the socio-economic and political complexities that point to the unfulfilled agenda of post-independence Kenyan nationhood. Owuor evokes the trope of death as signified in the pre-text epigram by Juan Rulfo that declares: *'You will hear the voice of my memories stronger than the voice of my death—that is, if death ever had a voice'* (Pedro Parama). Indeed, memories evoked by the death of the character Odidi Oganda control the development of the novel's intricate and intriguing plot. It is the memories associated with the death of Odidi Oganda that lead to the entanglements of individuals' personal lived narratives and national public narratives that invites a rhizomic reading of this novel. The diverse narratives that converge and diverge at certain nodal points, like those of a vector, indeed mirror the rhizome. How does this rhizomic structure enable the deployment of a dead body to simultaneously narrate and critique the unfulfilled agenda of independence and the unrealisable vision of nationhood in this novel?

Conceptualising the Rhizomic in the Reading of *Dust*

The complex and complicated narrative structuring of the novel *Dust* with multiplicities and multilayered plots and narrative modes of representation, necessarily requires a unique critical approach to unravel its variegated meanings. This approach can be found in Gilles Deleuze and Felix Guattari's (1987) understanding and interpretation of the metaphor of rhizome. Admittedly, the rhizomic simultaneously provides a register and a critical strategy of reading and generating meanings in this novel; a novel that both defies, undermines and resists linear assemblage and ordering of lived everyday and imagined experiences. The rhizome as a critical strategy as such enables the establishment of connections and intersections of disparate strata in the novel such as the killing of the fictitious character Odidi Oganda and the recognisable historical events such as the 2007 presidential elections, the 2007 post-election violence, the Mau Mau oath of silence among members of the Gĩkũyũ community during the emergency in the 1950s, and the assassinations of Pinto, Arwgings, Mboya, J.M. Kariuki and Mbae, among others. By deploying the rhizomic imagination and death/dead body to register experiences (history), Owuor seems, in the novel *Dust,* to participate in the project of national conscientisation; what Simatei (2001, 10) describes in a different context as follows: 'The novelist's relevance to society is attained through a conscious intervention in the unfolding of history; an intervention which, as a kind of artistic mission, is already over-determined by the inhuman politics of both colonial and postcolonial epochs.'

In registering the history that is already over-determined by inhuman politics of both colonial and postcolonial epochs, Owuor in *Dust* privileges a narrative structural strategy that in a way mirrors Deleuze and Guattari's (1987) notion of the rhizome as it has neither beginning, nor end, but always a middle (milieu) from which it grows and spills. The death of Odidi Oganda is apparently the medial point of this novel from which all the actions sprout, develop and disperse into the various micro-narratives and sub plots. Before delving deeper into the detailed nuances of how the rhizomic variously manifests in this novel, it is imperative to proffer a brief outline of the concept of rhizome as espoused by Deleuze and Guattari (1987) and how it lends itself as an effective theoretical prism for a critical reading of Owuor's novel *Dust* that grapples with the complexities and ironies of a nation's attempts to will itself into nationhood.

The rhizome is conceived as a philosophical concept, but which has also been widely deployed metaphorically in literary criticism. A rhizome is a form of plant-life which spreads, such as mushrooms or crabgrass, without a central root, spot or origination or logical pattern. 'The rhizome itself assumes very diverse forms, from ramified surface extension in all directions to concretion into bulbs and tubers' (Deleuze and Guattari 1987, 29). Deleuze and Guattari argue that they deploy this symbol of rootlessness because it opposes the traditional, rational and logical approach to knowledge. It is also construed as a rejection of the assumption of history of the dominant class. As a minor-oriented — rather than dominant-oriented — philosophical approach it is achieved by 'surveying and mapping' of those lost or dominated cultures, classes, sexes or races (Deleuze and Guttari 1987, 25–26). The narrative structure of *Dust* and its subject matter to a large extent seems to closely resonate with Deleuze and Guattari's (1987) description of the rhizome. *Dust* not only explores the experiences of the subalterns but more so the unrealised vision of post-independence Kenyan nationhood. The narrative structure of this novel is woven in a labyrinthine-like rhizome figure made only of lines that connect to a nodal point and to other nodal points. I also find quite illuminating Deleuze and Guattari's (1987) ideas of 'minor' language/'major' language; and, territorialisation and deterritorialisation in the writing and reading of the coming to birth of the Kenyan nation. However, because of the scope of this article, these inflections of rhizome will not be utilised.

The Meanings of Dust in the Novel *Dust*

The title, 'Dust', akin to rhizome, generates multiple meanings and implications. For instance, it could mean: fine, dry particles of matter; a cloud of fine, dry particles; particles of matter regarded as the result of disintegration (fabric that had fallen to dust over the centuries); Earth as especially when regarded as the substance of the grave implying both a beginning and an end that is from 'earth to earth, ashes to ashes, dust to dust' (*Book of Common*, 333); as the surface of the ground; a debased or despised condition; something of no worth; state of confusion, agitation, commotion (won't go back in until the dust settles); and 'you will see dust' also means real trouble, an idiom that was commonly used in Nairobi in the 1970s by teens. These multiple meanings of the word 'dust' are all implicated not only in the title of the novel but also in its fragmented narrative structure. It is the fragmentary structure — akin to 'blowing dust' — that ostensibly invites a rhizomic reading of unfulfilled desires for nationhood rendered through narrations of memories and re-memories of a dead body.

Dead Body and the (Hi)stories and Ironies of a Nation's Coming to Birth

The novel *Dust,* as already intimated, deploys death as a narrative organising structure because dead bodies are, in a sense, capable of generating multiple memories and narratives that are rhizome-like with different lines, connecting, intersecting and entangling at various nodes but still capable of flowing in multifaceted directions. As Peter Amuka (1995, 111–112) reminds us in his exhilarating essay "An Oral Reading of the Written: The example of Masira Kindaki":

> ... ironically, however, the most powerful and popular bodies are dead ones ... Abayo's dead body creates many more stories by the grave, in the grave and well after the burial ... With her death, Abayo's body becomes an embodiment of history or cultural tropes.

This resonates closely with Owuor's deployment of Odidi Oganda's death in the novel as it becomes an embodiment of history and narratives of the complexities of the willing of Kenyan nation into nationhood.

In the novel *Dust,* Owuor imaginatively uses death/dead body to dramatise and question the coming to birth of the Kenyan nation. Similar to fictional writings that deploy dead bodies and death that were mentioned at the beginning of this article, Owuor seems to insinuate that the death of the fictional character, Moses Ebesiwet Odidi Oganda, cannot be fully fathomed without making a backward glance, into the history of the coming to birth of the Kenyan nation. As such, fiction and real, lived experiences (history) are wittingly and inexorably intertwined through the imaginative possibilities offered by the rhizomic structure of the novel. The death of Odidi Oganda and the contested Kenya's presidential elections of 2007 seem to be entangled in a very complex and complicated way. In fact, understanding both Odidi Oganda's death and the post-election violence dramatised in the novel invites a total exposition of the personal, lived narratives of Odidi Oganda, his family and their associates and, more importantly, how these personal, lived narratives intersect with the public narratives of the coming to birth of Kenyan nation. Arguably, Odidi Oganda's death is deployed skilfully as a catalyst and a backdrop to lay bare the ironies of Kenya's attempt to will itself into nationhood. From a rhizomic reading, Odidi Oganda's death constitutes the middle of the novel where the narratives of both the Kenyan nation and his own family converge and diverge. Odidi's death generates narratives that resemble both centripetal and centrifugal forces always moving inwards and outwards, sometimes narrating his own experiences or those of the Kenyan nation. This approach is aptly captured by Deleuze and Parnent (1987) in their observation that:

> … it is a matter of record that what is interesting takes place 'in the middle'. And literature, more so than any other form of discourse, has potential to explore the middle. In this way, literature can explore the 'event'. A commonsense narrative conceives of events in a conventional way; an event like a battle, has locatable beginning and an end, and is constituted by a series of actors … events, even great events like battles, are much more enigmatic: Any event is a fog of a million droplets. [(Deleuze and Parnent 1987, 65 cited in Buchan and Marks (2000, 2)]

In the novel both the death of Odidi Oganda and the 2007 post-election violence in Kenya are the events, fog-like, which trigger multiplicities of narratives, like droplets that attempt to explain the impediments to the realisation of the project of Kenyan's nationhood. This resonates with Simatei's (2001, 35) observation that, 'To express the irony of Independence, i.e., the experience of Independence as a suspension rather than fulfilment of the agenda of, Kibera in *Voices in the Dark* presents the architects of Uhuru as the tragic victims of the historical moment they have helped to create.'

The death of Odidi Oganda and the post-election violence are apt exemplars of this tragedy of suspended agenda of Independence. The narrator clearly accentuates this:

> A twist deforms Ajany's full lips. *Here.* The evidence. They are descendants of a lineage of Living Dead. Breathing in, she shifts her body to stare at a beige coffin, habitat of the new and unquiet dead on a day when distorted election results will set bucolic country afire. The outside world is drenched with human noises of accusations and counteraccusations, election rigging, and the miracle of mathematical votes that multiply and divide themselves. But within their world, in a self-contained, haunted compound with its lone, misshapen grevillea tree upon which a purple-blue bird tweets, and where death prowls at half past three, Ajany bends forward to listen to and for her brother, Odidi, whose story-words had created vessels that always carried her into safe border. (Owuor 2013, 19)

Deploying this rhizomic narration strategy Owuor wittingly brings out the ironies of independence in the way that the novel recalls the tragic experiences of the colonial period in the post-independence epoch. The narrator superimposes the personal narrative of Odidi Oganda's death onto that of the 2007 presidential elections and the violence that ensued, clearly insinuating that the two events are interconnected and interwoven.

Having located the novel *Dust* within the realm of the rhizomatic-book, the focus now turns to how this rhizomatic structure offers the possibilities of engaging with the project of coming to birth of the postcolonial Kenyan nation. The novel's rhizomatic structuring seems to bequeath Owour the poetic licence to comment liberally on and critique the project of the coming to birth of the Kenyan nation through various connections and interconnections made amongst the rhizome-like narratives of the fictitious characters and the real, lived experiences that inform the history of Kenya as a nation in the making. The story of Nyipir's life, as in all rhizome-like books, begins in the middle. The middle is the death of his son, Odidi Oganda, killed in Nairobi by the police.

However, to understand the meaning of Odidi Oganda's death entails the laying bare of his father's life as it intersects with the coming to birth of the Kenyan nation. Nyipir's life, like the rhizome line(s) intersects at various nodal points with the larger history of Kenya. It is through these intersections of Nyipiri's own personal history and those of the Kenyan nation that Owuor wittingly critiques the unfulfilled agenda of Independence when the founding leader of the nation proclaimed the slogan *nyakua* (Owuor 2013, 26). As a rhizomatic-book, neither stories — of Nyipir Oganda or of Kenyan nation in *Dust* — follows a linear plot as both shift forwards and backwards throughout the novel. The events, depicted as being in the present moment, such as Odidi Oganda's death and the post-election violence, can only be fathomed through the evocation of memories evoked by this death. Nyipir's memories and re-memories, as he prepares the funeral of his son, Odidi Oganda, shifts between his own personal experiences and the history of the coming to birth of the Kenyan nation. Through fragmented short memories, Owuor ably manages to explore Nyipir's entire life and the history of the Kenyan nation.Nyipir's memories take him back to his childhood and how the departure of his father unsettled the lives of his entire family. The difficulties and circumstances that he faced at home compelled him to flee from his home, eventually ending up in Central Kenya highlands. It is here that his personal life gets entangled with the struggle for independence. He participates in the clandestine burial of Mau Mau followers killed by the colonial government during interrogation and witnesses the taking of the oath of silence by the Mau Mau followers as well as the murder of those who collaborated with the colonial government or declined to take the oath. What astounds Nyipir is how this culture of silence, initiated through the oath-taking rituals, would later become a major defining characteristic of post-independence Kenya.

For Nyipir, it is this culture of silence that started in the pre-independence period that will undermine the realisation of Kenya's sense of nationhood. As he digs the grave to bury his son, Nyipir realises that the killings, such as that of his son and of politicians who had been assassinated, are part of this coterminous culture. The following shifts and counter shifts in his reverie revealing the past, present and anticipated future of Kenyan nation suffices to illustrate:

> To protect the new post-independence citizen children, parents like him repainted illusions of a 'future Kenya,' while shouting out words of the national anthem as if volume alone would recreate reality. *Nyakua*. Mouths, ears, and eyes shut, parents partitioned

> sorrow, purchased more silences and waited for the 'better Kenya' to turn up.
>
> Nyipir's daily covenants with silence had all of a sudden lost their weight. Today the voices of the dead-providing-their own-witness take over his thoughts with a sound track—Babu Kabaselleh's 'Lek Wuonda, to remind Nyipir that the dying started long ago. Before Pio, Tom, J.M., Argwings, before the red, black, green, and white flag fluttered one mid-night December ...
>
> Stillness. Then Nyipir speaks.' A man I knew used to say *Ona icembe riugi ni rituhaga* (Even a sharp *jembe*/hoe can get blunt with constant use) before we dug the graves. (Owuor 2013, 46–47)

Nyipir, before independence, had collaborated with the colonial administration through his relationship with Hugh Bolton who recruited him into the police force and for whom he worked. It is through his relationship with Bolton that he had found himself in the Northern Frontier and where he named the place *Wuoth Ogik* (the end of the journey). It is significant that it is as a result of Odidi Oganda's death that we get insight into this past life of Nyipir, Akai Lokorijom and Bolton Hugh. Nyipir kills Bolton to protect Akai to whom he gets married and begets two children, Odidi Oganda and Ajany. His killing of Bolton is part of the litany of deaths that had remained hidden. Symbolically, the killing of Bolton signifies the death of colonialism. It also symbolises Nyipir's active participation in the struggle for freedom and independence.

The relationship between Akai and Bolton can be interpreted as a microcosm of the imbalanced relationship between the colonised and the coloniser. Bolton exploits Akai who acts as his mistress. He uses her to fulfil his sexual desires and fantasy as captured in the nude portraits that he takes of Akai.

Nyipir's personal lived experiences and those of the public are further revealed when he is depicted enthusiastically and optimistically, playing a major role in the independence celebration of the new Kenyan nation. He was one of the key celebrants in the rituals that marked the coming to birth of the Kenyan nation. However, through the use of short memories, Nyipir reveals how the agenda of Independence of the new nation had been suspended way before the chaos of 2007/2008 post-election violence and the death of his son, Odidi Oganda. Indeed, the chaos was simply an affirmation of that fact. I reproduce this long quote from the novel as it significantly captures the unfulfilled agenda of Independence, the betrayal of the sense of nationhood depicted in the quotes rhizomic fragmentary structure through the deliberate splitting of words, phrases and sentences:

> Today
>
> The past's beckon is persistent.
>
> From the air, Nyipir peers down at the expanding abyss. His country, his home, is ripping itself apart. Stillborn ballot revolution. These 2007 elections were supposed to be simple, the next small jump into a light-filled Kenyan future. Everything had instead disintegrated into a single, unending howl by the nation's unrequited dead. This country, this haunted ideal, all its poor, broken promises. Nyipir watches, armpits damp. A view of ground-lit smoke. Dry lips. His people had never set their nation on

fire before.

On the ground, that night, in a furtive ceremony, beneath a half-moon, a chubby man will mutter an oath that will render him the president of a burning, dying country. The deed will add fuel on an already-out-of-control national grieving.

Nyipir turns from the window,
He is flying home with his children.
Yet he is alone.
Memories are solitary ghosts.
He lets them in, traveling with them.

Downcountry.
December 12, 1963
Lengees, a soldier, hoisted a red, black, green, and white flag up in a park. The flag collected sparks, and visions drifting like clouds. In that arena of spectacle, Nyipir Oganda had led a cavalcade, lugging a smaller red, black, green, and white flag while riding on high-stepping black horse. He had shrieked as if expelling a fiend: 'Eyeeeeeees left.'
Clop-clop-clop-clop. Hooves and blurring vision. Men on a podium, some who he thought had died. Two men he knew had pounded other men to death. Another had been detained for his own safety and been supplied with a stream of world literature and unlovely comfort women, one of whom he married. He had focused on one man —Tom Joseph Mboya, who colored in the red, green, white, and black flag. He had, years before, scoured the landscape and found promising souls that he sent to America to study, experience, and then come back home with transcendent dreams. The Leader of the Nation had tilted his head at the tracker-policeman carrying the Kenya flag, a dark man on a black horse. In his sweaty palms, the flag had almost slipped as Nyipir had bellowed, 'Eyeeeeeees front!' A mosaic people had cheered. Wanderers, cattlemen, camel herders, fishermen, and hunters, dreamers, strangers, gatherers and farmers, trading nations, empire builders, and the forgetful. Such were the people for whom Nyipir had carried the new Kenya flag. There was also the anthem created from a Pokomo mother's lullaby:

Eh Mungu Nguvu Yetu
Ilete Baraka kwetu
Haki iwe ngao na mlinzi ….

O God of all creation, Bless this land and nation, Justice be our shield and defender …

Blended cultures, intoxicating fusion—the new, revised Kenya. Bead *kofia* on his head, cloaked, fly-whisk flicking, the Leader spoke. His voice was a bass drum. Glory! Good! Forgiveness! Education! Work hard! Nyipir had tended the fire-lit euphoria inside his body. *Harambee! Harambee*! A nation brought to task in clarion call that had hauled steel across the land and built a railway. The national summons. Response —a howled Eehhhhh!

But then came the fear.

It split words into smaller and smaller fragments until words became secret, suffocating, and silent. No one cried when voracious, frenzied seizing of lives began. A new word slithered into the landscape—*Nyakua*: plunder, possess. Entitled brigandage. But it was cleansed to mean 'hard work'. In the nation, slow horror, as if all had woken up to a vision of violating, crowing ghouls crowding their beds. Nyipir remembers how bodies started to stoop to contain the shame, the loss, the eclipse. Such eyes-turned-inward silences so that when bodies started showing up mutilated and truly dead, the loudest protests were created out of whispers. To protect new post-independence citizen children, like most new Kenyan parents denying soul betrayals, Nyipir built

> illusions of another Kenya, shouting out words of national anthem when he could as if the volume alone would remove the rust eating into national hopes. Keeping mouths, ears, and eyes shut, parents had partitioned sorrow, purchased even more silence, and promised a 'better future' (Owuor 2013, 24–26).

Through the deployment of these short memories, which according to Deleuze and Guattari (1987, 37) 'is in no way subject to a law of contiguity or immediacy to its object; it can act at distance, come or return long after, but always under conditions of discontinuity, rupture and multiplicity' implicates the slogan *nyakua* that was proclaimed in 1963 by the founding father of the nation and which now becomes a catalyst for the post-election violence of 2007/008 as well as the death of Odidi Oganda. From Owuor's narrator, it seems that the problems that beset the coming to birth of the post-independence Kenyan nation can be traced to this slogan that putatively suspended the genuine project of nation-building and, instead, created a culture of fear, silence, corruption and plunder. The narrator contemplates it thus: 'The death of Odidi reminds him of the death of Tom Mboya and how that particular death undermined the project of national building and nationhood' (Owuor 2013, 271).

The narrator reveals that:

> Nyipir had lost his Kenya on July 5, 1969, in Nairobi, when Tom Mboya was assassinated. The murder was the culmination of fears, swirling rumors, the meaning of clandestine oaths that made the rest of the country enemy territory to be owned. It was the purpose of the silences that had started before. (Owuor 2013, 271)

It is interesting to note that the death of Mboya and the 2007 post-election bear close resemblance to the colonial atrocities and deaths that Nyipir witnessed in Fort Hall during the emergency and are all adversely implicated in deferment of coming to birth of the Kenyan nation. For instance, the consequences of Mboya's death complicates the realisation of the agenda of the independence that envisaged a united nation. The narrator observes that:

> This death created a fissure in the nation, as if it had split apart its own soul …
>
> After Mboya, everything that could die in Kenya did, even schoolchildren standing in front of a hospital that the Leader of the nation had come to open. A central province was emptied of a people who were renamed cockroaches and 'beasts from the west.' But nobody would acknowledge the exiles or citizens who did not make it out of the province before they were destroyed. Oaths of profound silences—secret shots in a slithering civil war. (Owuor 2013, 272)

It is through rhizomic imaginary that Owour links up all these variegated events, beginning with the death of Odidi Oganda and the post-election violence to show how the agenda of Independence and concomitantly the project of nationhood have persistently been deferred. The narrator proclaims that: 'Until the day

Nyipir washed his son's naked unmoving body, and heard how a grieving Kenya, to receive a new year, 2008, had set itself on fire' (Owuor 2013, 275).

The novel ends in an interesting way when all the main characters' rhizomatic-like narratives converge in Wuoth Ogik. Here all the characters' secrets are laid bare, showing how their narratives are entangled into each other's. But there is a sense also in which the lines of their narratives intersect with that of the nation in turmoil. As Kofi Annan strikes a peace deal leading to a coalition government, these characters also reveal their deep held secrets, eventually leading to reconciliation and healing. But the irony is that though this place of convergence is called Wuoth Ogik, after revelations and confessions of their secret lives, all the characters like rhizome-lines take flight to go and begin new lives elsewhere. As such these narratives like rhizomic-lines can be described in terms of vectors ... 'meant to converge at a volatile juncture, but ... sustained, as an open equilibrium of moving parts each with its own trajectory' (Deleuze and Guattari 1987, xiv).

Just as the reconciliation at the national level after the violence is anticipated to mark a new beginning in the life of the nation, so are those of the individual characters. The heavy rain that pours at the end of the novel seems to allude to the biblical floods in the book of Genesis that washed out the old sinful world and ushered in a new one.

Conclusion

The possibilities that accrue in the rhizomatic-book as philosophically articulated by Deleuze and Guattari provides illuminating insights for critical transactions with Owuor's novel of multiplicities and multilayeredness. Using the rhizome as an interpretive mode enables a reading of difficulties of the coming to birth of the Kenyan nation through the fictional narratives of Nyipir's family and those associated with them. The rhizome as lines that intersect at various nodal points makes it possible to connect the personal narratives of the individual characters with public narratives of the nation such as the chaos witnessed after the contested presidential elections in 2007. The rhizome as a strategy enables the author to use death to evoke memories which reveal the problematic history of the making of the Kenyan nation. The death of Odidi Oganda, gunned down in the streets of Nairobi, forces his family to face secrets from their past, secrets entangled with the colonial and postcolonial history of Kenya.

Disclosure Statement

No potential conflict of interest was reported by the author.

Funding

The author(s) reported there is no funding associated with the work featured in this article.

References

Amuka, Peter. 1995. "An Oral Reading of the Written: The example of *Masira Kindaki.*" In *Creative Use of Language in Kenya*, edited by Kwadzo Senanu and Drid Williams, 106–114. Nairobi: Jomo Kenyatta Foundation.

Book of Common Prayers and Administration of the Sacraments and Other Rites and Ceremonies of the Church. Protestant Episcopal Church in the USA.

Buchanan, Ian, and John Marks, eds. 2000. *Deleuze and Literature*. Edinburg: Edinburg University Press.

Deleuze, Gilles and Guattari, Felix. 1987. *A Thousand Plateaus: Capitalism and Schizophrenia*. (Transl. Brian Massumi). London/Minneapolis: University of Minnesota.

Imbuga, Francis. 1976. *Betrayal in the City*. Nairobi: Heinemann.

Owuor, Adhiambo. Yvonne. 2013. *Dust*. New York. Alfred Knopf.

Scott, Denis. 1986. *An Echo in the Bone*. London: Longman.

Simatei, Tirop, Peter. 2001. *The Novel and the Politics of Nation Building in East Africa*. Bayreuth: Bayreuth University Press.

Wright, Richard. 1940. *Native Son*. Chicago: Harper and Brothers.

The Use of Ellipsis as a Narrative Technique in Yvonne Owuor's *Dust*

Jennifer Muchiri

ABSTRACT
This paper reads the use of ellipsis as a narrative technique in Yvonne Owuor's *Dust*. The paper interrogates the deployment of ellipsis in the novel as a strategy for contesting notions of homogeneity at different levels. Through the use of ellipsis, the novel constantly ruptures its own form, but which inherently calls for continuity. These gaps invite the reader to be a co-creator in the narrative and, therefore, participate in imagining the community, nation, and the history in the novel. I argue that the elliptical narration in the novel is significant in uncovering silences, gaps, secrets, omissions, and shadows which constitute the writer's imaginary and portrayal of Kenya.

Introduction

Yvonne Adhiambo Owuor's novel, *Dust* (2013), is her second work, the others being "Weight of Whispers" (2006), a short story, and *The Dragonfly Sea* (2019), a novel. In *Dust*, Owuor tells the story of Ajany, a young woman whose brother, Odidi, has disappeared in mysterious circumstances. Ajany embarks on a journey to find her brother and in the process discovers that he is dead. Her journey to search for the 'truth' about Odidi's disappearance and death leads her to unearth other unknown stories about her parents, family, and the country.

My working definition of ellipsis is the omission from a sentence of a word or words that would conventionally be necessary for comprehension of a text but whose absence does not detract from the reader's understanding because the text can be understood from the context. Such omissions can be indicated in various forms such as directly by way of the elliptical three dots (…) or indirectly through such signs as silences, contractions, asyndeta, and paratactical sentences.

Dust presents us with a narrative that attempts to recreate and reconstruct the history of Kenya. Like other women writers in post-independence nations, Owuor is involved in a process of 'claiming a historical validity for the ordinary [by situating her work] alongside, and overlapping with, conventional narratives of a national, public history' (Boehmer 2005, 218). Her novel digs into the memories of characters in an effort to recreate individual and collective histories of families, communities, and a nation. The novel is an allegory of postcolonial Kenya. The writer demonstrates that history can be erratic and constructing it from memory even more problematic since memory can be elusive.

Through ellipsis and related literary forms such as repetition, omission, repression, and truncation, this novel emphatically suggests that history is not homogenous. The narrative and characters demonstrate that the making of a nation is not a simple process and neither does it follow a linear pattern. Instead, the process is a painstaking one that requires meticulous digging into the past and into citizens' lives to unearth the untold stories — the silenced sections of the nation's existence. This paper focuses on ellipsis as the central narrative technique that the writer employs to underscore the gaps, silences, omissions, absences, secrets, and non-naming that characterise modern Kenya's history. It looks at the fragmented narration and the non-linear plot in the novel as symbolic representations of the disjointed nature of the postcolonial Kenyan nation and the culture of silence that permeates through the nation.

Notions of Ellipsis

The novel begins with a cataphoric introduction to a character whose name is only revealed later in the narrative — 'He leaps over two fire-painted blossoms resting on the stark cracked city pavement' (7). The delayed mention of Odidi keeps his name 'secret' at the beginning. The non-naming of the character at the beginning of the story sets in motion a series of absences and silences in the narrative. The neologism of 'late-Christmas-season' and 'orange-and-black' (7) indicates a sense of absence of an appropriate English word to describe the season and the butterflies' colour which therefore requires the narrator to create or coin new words. The idea of vagueness is further enhanced by the diction in the opening paragraph. Words such as 'echo,' 'violet shade,' 'smog-encrusted,' 'thicket,' and 'still-distant night' (7) create a mood of shadows and absence of light which indicate that here is something that is either being hidden or is absent.

The short sentences, some consisting of only two words, create a staccato tone in the narration and indicate a sense of omission and, therefore, urgency: '*Hao*! There they are. *Waue*! Kill them. *Wezi*! Thieves. Odidi runs' (7). The narrator does not clearly state who 'they' refers to at this point, again creating the sense of secrecy and absence through cataphora. The lexical deviation in the form of foreign words (in Kiswahili) introduces a kind of multiplicity of voices in the narrative without making it obvious that there is a crowd involved in this particular incident. The prologue and introduction of the novel thus introduce us to a narrative steeped in ellipsis, which manifests itself in various forms.

The non-linear plot, with large sections of the story narrated through flashbacks, gives the novel a staccato, elliptical nature too. We meet Odidi running away from a mob that is baying for his blood and we are transported, through a flashback, to some of the events that have led to the present moment. We experience a very short encounter between Odidi and the Somali warlord. Their conversation is hurried, held in short sentences and one-word answers, almost as if they dare not reveal everything that they know.

The sudden shift of time from the events of three weeks before to the present moment of imminent danger creates a gap in the narration. The suspense is amplified by the fact that it has not yet been revealed why the crowd wants Odidi dead. The moment is a tense one and this tension is enhanced by the use of a combination of short sentences, foreign words, onomatopoeia, neologism of compound words, and the unconventional one-word sentences:

> Now.
> '*Waue*!' The pursuing Nairobi mob howls.
> *Odidi runs.*
> *Not feeling the ground. Soaring.*
> *Swish, zip, pop, rattle.*
> Bullets.
> Grunt, *thud*. A man falls.
> *Ratatatata* ... Screams.
> Odidi runs.
> Tears flood. Terror-rage-love fuse.
> The fallen ones are his men.
> Guilt. Fury. Sorrow. (8–9)

The combination of literary devices creates a sense of confusion, vagueness, and secrecy. The repetition of the words 'Odidi runs' eleven times in a span of two pages (9–11) indicates the presence of fear and mystery which contribute to the elliptical nature of the narrative.

As Odidi runs away from his pursuers the narrator allows us to listen in to an interior monologue as he recollects his memories of growing up in Wuoth Ogik, which intersperses them with his present thoughts about death. He is running away physically from the mob and psychologically from his past. Since this past is still unrevealed, the narrative exists in a kind of partial darkness, which is consistent with the 'shadow and regrets' (9) that Odidi seems to be running away from. The moment immediately after Odidi is shot is described in a series of short sentences that creates an atmosphere of tension, fear, urgency, pain, and the desire to escape:

> Odidi limps.
>
> He grips his shattered right shoulder. Protrusion of bone. Blood trail. Trickle from his mouth. It is said that in the throes of battle dying men cry out for their mothers. *Akai-ma*, Odidi groans. She wards off ghouls and bad night entities, wrestles God, casts ancient devils into hell before their time, and kicks aside sea waves so her son will

> pass unhindered. Akai-ma. Throb in the back of Odidi's left leg. Searing that eats the base of his spine. Damp from his chest. (11)

Odidi's thoughts after he is shot are narrated elliptically with a to-and-fro shift from the present to the past and back to the present through flashbacks. As the pain goes through his body, in the present, his thoughts are about his family — sister, mother, Galgalu — in the past. While the past is recalled in a continuous prose, the present is narrated in short, encrypted sentences, made mostly of one word, and presented in a staccato mode that deviates from conventional prose. (12–13) The narrator hints at information regarding Odidi's 'ownership' of his sister Ajany but it is only through a foreshadow because the real circumstances under which Odidi and Galgalu 'retrieved [Ajany] from the fixed gaze of five waiting vultures' (13) is only revealed later in the narrative. The silence regarding these circumstances, in which Akai-ma had left her daughter in the desert to die, symbolises the secrets that surround these characters' lives. The shift in narrative time, as well as the narration in pseudo-verse, symbolise the haziness and confusion that mark the moment of Odidi's transition from life to death. It is a moment characterised by shadows and silences because the narrator is yet to reveal the cause of Odidi's fleeing.

There is also, together with the various flashbacks, a shift in setting from 'a bitumen-smelling potholed backstreet' in Nairobi where Odidi lies dead, to the 'desert essences — dung, salt, milk, smoke, herbs, and ghee, the yearning for rain' (15), the home he longs for. The physical distance between the two places, and the psychological import of this distance for Odidi, create a kind of gap between what was, what is, and what could have been. While the idea of home, for Odidi, is 'the cream of hot milk of their animals, ... chewed grass, slime layered goat tongues on skin ... ,' (15) unfortunately, it becomes 'a bitumen-smelling backstreet.' Instead of getting to throw himself into his mother's arms, what Odidi sees is 'a shadow' (15). This idea of unfulfilled dreams is one that cuts across the entire narrative. The moment of Odidi's 'departure' is, therefore, marked by shadows, emptiness, and silences which are communicated through a series of short phrases, sentences, and single but weighty words: '*What do you want*? Hollow hunger. Perpetual thirst. Here I am. The thing smiles. Odidi understands. If you touch her ... Odidi shivers. Leave her alone. Cold tears. ... Please. ... Not her fault, Odidi pleads. I'm here' (15).

Odidi and Ajany's visit to the forbidden caves, also narrated through a flashback, carries with it a sense of secrets and mysteries. The vivid description of the caves portrays a kind of unseen shadow which portends an unspoken danger or serves as a sign of lurking evil. The children's discovery of a human skeleton intensifies the sense of secrecy in the caves and, symbolically, in the lives of the characters. The skull is missing some teeth and has sunken sockets, signifying an absence, an incompleteness, since the children do not know who the skeleton belongs to or how it got to be in the caves. The narrator foreshadows the narrative of Hugh Bolton, whose remains are in the cave, as a way of indicating the multiplicity of secrets and silences that the narrative carries. The skeleton itself is a symbol of secrets, as is the cave in which it is found. That the narrator refers to the skeleton as a 'thing' (16) portrays the absence of life, a loss of its humanity, and the fact that having been thrown away or abandoned in a cave, the skeleton lacks an identity. In essence, however, the skeleton lacks an identity only because the people who put it in the cave were trying to erase that identity, to hide the truth about Bolton ever having been in or around Wuoth Ogik.

The presence of the skeleton, thus, not only symbolises a hint of the proverbial skeletons in the closet of the characters in the novel but also foreshadows the series of secrets and absences through death in the rest of the narrative. The mysterious skeleton instils so much fear in Ajany that she can only talk about it in a stammer: "Didi, I dream of … of … Obaro … Oba … ' (17). In a sense, therefore, ellipsis is used in this instance to portray fear in the individual and the nation; fear of the past, the present, and the unknown future.

As Odidi is about to die he realises that he and his gang members have been set up by police officers whom they have been paying to turn a blind eye to their criminal activities. At that moment Odidi experiences a mixture of pain, betrayal, bitterness, guilt, sorrow, loneliness, and shame all at once. The narrator describes Odidi's troubled psychological and physical state using elliptical short sentences to capture the intensity of the moment:

> Shit!
> Odidi understood.
> A set up … .
> Sorrow is a universe.
> Guilt.
> Shame at being fooled. …
> Such is loneliness.
> Tears.
> Electric chill-pain.
> Odidi shivers.
> Blood. (20)

Odidi's mind is in turmoil and the ellipsis aptly captures this state of being.

The cataphoric introduction to Ajany in chapter one presents us with a character who feels empty and lost after the death of her brother, Odidi. The absence of Odidi in a way creates an absence of self in Ajany. Ajany sees her father as misplaced in the city when they are preparing to take Odidi's body home for burial. The narrator reveals Ajany's thoughts about her father who she sees as having an 'efficient out-of-place-ness' (24). This neologism describing Nyipir's presence underlines the secrets and circumstances surrounding his life, which are yet to be revealed, but which Ajany has an inkling of. This would explain why Ajany's thoughts, which are clearly bitter ones because 'bile in [her] throat burns, dissolving her screaming,' (24) lead to an unexplained ellipsis:

'I hate ... ' (24). The omission of the pronoun 'her' and the elliptical presentation of her feelings at that moment foreshadow the many secrets in her and her family's existence.

Odidi's death is significant because it allows for the interrogation of the narrative of death in the nation. Odidi is representative of postcolonial Kenya which must look back to her past to examine the various deaths, physical or metaphorical, that have marked her past. The narrator alludes to the deaths of 'prophets named Pio, Tom, Argwings, Ronald, Kungu, Josiah, Ouko, Mbae' referring to them as the 'disappeared unknown' as a way of recalling the assassinations of several Kenyans whose deaths have remained unresolved, shrouded in mystery and secrecy, because 'national doors slammed over vaults of secrets' (28).

As Nyipir thinks about the death of his son, snippets of his feelings lead to thoughts about the state of the country and what ails her. Odidi's death is narrated against the backdrop of the bungled 2007 general elections and the violence that erupted thereafter. The country is described as 'ripping itself apart [after a] stillborn ballot revolution' (29). Nyipir is a worried Kenyan seeing as 'his people had never set their nation on fire before' (29). The pain and grief of an individual mourning the death of his son is narrated side by side with that of a nation grieving 'a burning, dying country' (29).

The story of Nyipir's family is presented as an allegory of Kenya. Each of the characters in the novel is searching for something but their separate lives are bound by a common history. As Mikhail Bakhtin says, 'out of common time of collective life emerge separate individual life-sequences, individual fates' (1981, 214). The novel alludes to Kenya's history of colonialism and the coming of independence by telling the story of Nyipir whose life is part of that history. Nyipir had been present at the dawn of independence when the different peoples of Kenya had cheered the rise of the new Kenyan flag. The narrator captures the unity of the nation at independence by painting the different people that welcomed independence — 'wanderers, cattlemen, camel herders, fishermen and hunters, dreamers, strangers, gatherers and farmers, trading nations, empire builders, and the forgetful' (30). The mention of the different categories of Kenyans who welcomed independence is a representation of the great hope and dream that the nation had then, which is symbolised by the words of the leader (an allusion to Jomo Kenyatta), and which are presented in an elliptical series: 'Glory! Goodness! Forgiveness! Education!' (30).

The shattering of the dream of independence is communicated in just one line, which serves as a bridge in the shift of time from the days of independence to the present — 'But then came the fear' (30). This short sentence opens the narrative to point to the various ills that define postcolonial Kenya. The postcolonial government instilled so much fear in the citizens that 'words became secret, suffocating, and silent' (30) and the narrative of death started. The narrator alludes to theft of national resources and political assassinations which happened after independence and decries the silence with which Kenyans responded to these evils. No one dared speak against the state and even when citizens were killed, 'the loudest protests were created out of whispers' (30). The new nation was characterised by fear which led to silence. The dream of independence thus became an illusion as citizens maintained silence despite the ills around them; they learnt the art of 'keeping mouths, ears, and eyes shut [while] parents had partitioned sorrow, purchased even more silence, and promised a "better future"' (30). The narrator underscores the irony of promising a better future yet they are silent about the threatened present. Wole Soyinka (2004), writing about a people's intimacy with fear, argues that 'a notable aspect of all-pervasive fear is that it induces a degree of loss of self-apprehension: a part of one's self has been appropriated, a level of consciousness, and this may even lead to a reduction in one's self esteem — in short, a loss of inner dignity' (8). Soyinka may have been writing about the individual, but his thoughts apply to the collective as well. There is a sense in which the fear in postcolonial Kenya undermines individual and collective dignity among its citizens. Fearful people care the less about the present or future well-being of the nation.

Ellipsis and the use of short sentences aid the narrative's shift in tense, time — both historical and chronological — setting, and focus. For instance, the narration about Nyipir's loss of a son and the period of independence suddenly shifts to the arrival of Isaiah Bolton in just one sentence — 'now here he was in Kenya' (35). This short sentence introduces not just a new character in the narrative but also compounds the secrets of the story. Isaiah arrives without notice, looking for information about his father. The narrator describes his search in ellipsis: 'Cold and red: the color of grasping at air, of hoping to be found or chosen or wanted for more than a season, for more than what he owned. Cold and cracked: the impossible-to-reach broken parts of the soul. Cold and hard: rebuilding' (35). The elliptical sentences, combined with repetition and neologism, communicates an individual's (Isaiah's) sense of loss, search, and abandonment which are, in essence, the collective feelings of Kenyans. The sense of emptiness that the individual (Nyipir and Isaiah) experiences mirrors that of the postcolonial nation.

Akai and Ajany feel similar pain and loss; Akai for the death of a son and Ajany the loss of a brother and protector and the rejection of a mother. Watching her mother cuddle Odidi's body, Ajany is so overwhelmed by grief and pain of alienation that she cannot think or express herself coherently. Her thoughts are communicated in faltering sentences which reflect her disturbed mind:

> A churning heat, like a heartburn with a rusty aftertaste, grows in Ajany's gullet. *Cry*, Ajany tells herself. An ugly jealousy, of wanting to be the dead one held by her mother, being invoked to life by such sounds. Shame. Akai's whimper. *Cry*, Ajany tells herself. Watches her brother limp in her mother's arms. Live, she commands Odidi. But her eyes are dry. (41)

Akai cannot believe that her only son is dead. The sight of the coffin momentarily paralyses her and she cannot speak clearly. Her feelings and thoughts are presented in staccato mode to demonstrate her shock and helplessness.

> 'Show. Me.'
> No time. No space. ... She rocks her son, strokes his face, rocks her son. Odidi, she croons. Odidi, wake up. Son. Listen. Ebewesit. I'm calling you.
> To name something is to bring it to life. ...
> Akai-ma moans furiously. ... 'Take me. Here, you thing, take me.' ...
> She screeches, 'Don't. Touch. Me. You. Don't. Touch ... Don't.' (40-41)

The disjointed sentences express Ajany and Akai's anger, frustration, and powerlessness in the face of death. The two characters' direct address to Odidi, who is dead, acts as an apostrophe that communicates an absence, a gap in their lives. Akai's mental instability is triggered by pain and it symbolises an ailing nation — a mentally ill nation. The nation is unstable due to the burden of pain it carries which citizens often do not talk about. Like Akai, many Kenyans are 'unsettled ghosts [who] have set the land afire and a gang of men [who] are howling and dancing down a city street, dangling a man's cut-off head' (46). 'Unsettled ghosts' is a metaphor for the disquiet, restlessness in the country, due to the many Kenyans cruelly killed or affected by the violence that erupted in 2008 yet these actions remain unavenged. The concept of ghosts evokes a sense of emptiness and unwanted memories which are what the novel is about.

Nyipir represents certain elements of colonial and postcolonial history of Kenya. He holds 'covenants with silence' (51) but the death of Odidi reopens the vaults of silence. The narrator exposes the motif of death and dying as part of Kenya's history, noting that 'the dying started long ago. Before Pio, Tom, J. M., Argwings, before the red, black, green, and white flag fluttered one midnight in December' (51). Nyipir's thoughts are cryptic but the allusion to political assassinations, which were shrouded in mystery, lends credence to the narrative's concern with the evils of colonialism and the state of the postcolony. Nyipir holds secrets about the murders that were committed by the crown before independence just like the postcolonial state keeps silent about the murders of political leaders after independence. Nyipir's stream of consciousness leads him to hear 'voices of the dead-providing-their-own-witness,' an indication that the secrets of the past are bound to be revealed. The neologism is symbolic of a new state of being; hope that the truth will emerge to save a dying nation.

The fragments of Nyipir's thoughts foreshadow secrets, which are underscored by the use of lexical deviation in Gikuyu, a language that is neither Dholuo nor Ngaturkana - which Nyipir's family speak — nor Kiswahili, the national and one of the official languages, nor English, the primary language of the text. The Gikuyu proverb that Nyipir repeatedly utters, *'Ona icembe riugi ni rituhaga'* (a sharp axe eventually gets blunt) (52) creates a sense of evasiveness which shows the presence of secrets. The proverb, loosely translated, refers to the idea of change, that over time, even secrets get revealed or discovered. Yet, the presence of a different language not only introduces to the novel a sense of heteroglossia, which enhances the artistry of the novel, but it also points to the historical context that informs the story. As Bakhtin argues, the novel, as a genre, can comprise of 'a diversity of social speech types (sometimes even diversity of languages) and a diversity of individual voices, artistically organized' (1981, 262).

The secrecy of Nyipir's past life is carried through the use of words and phrases that indicate an absence, gap, or unwillingness to reveal the truth. For instance, the man who taught Nyipir that proverb remains unnamed (a man I used to know). He offers no explanation about the graves they dug in the past and Ajany only hears the phrase *'dug the graves'* (52). As Nyipir hacks at the ground, there is 'nothing more to add. Glut of shadows. Shadows of phantoms.' As Ajany ponders her father's words she thinks about her 'disappearing mother, heaving silences, and the desire to vomit out a nameless anguish' (52). Words such as 'nothing,' 'shadows,' 'phantoms,' 'nameless' carry with them a sense of ellipsis because they indicate something unspoken. The repetition of the question 'what endures' (52) throughout the narrative indicates the silence with which the postcolonial nation responds to the ills that assail her.

The characters' memories of the past are interspersed with thoughts about the present through the use of flashbacks. The narrator severally uses the one-word sentence 'now' (57; 59) to indicate a shift from the past to the present and in the process indicate movement and change. Ajany gets the strength to live in the present by replaying, in her mind, her conversations with Odidi when they were younger. The two of them have a desire to go away from Wuoth Ogik but they are afraid that they do not have the means to do so. The old house contains secrets that they do not understand, and no one is willing to unravel those secrets. The mystery around their home is reflected in their conversation which clearly indicates their distress as they speak in incomplete sentences:

> Odidi said, "Jany, you'll paint.'
> She had shaken her head.
> 'Can't.'
> 'Can.'
> 'Don't know how to start.'
> 'Try.'
> 'Everything burned.'
> 'Silly, paint a river out of Wuoth Ogik. Then paint an ocean and a ship, and inside the ship, me and you going Far Away.' (57)

The elliptical omission of the personal pronouns in the above conversation is symbolic not only the characters' inclination to detach themselves from the heart of things for fear of the unknown but also their desire to break free of the secrets that abide in their home and family hence their wish to go to an unnamed place they call 'Far Away.'

Their parents do not help in the children's search for answers. If anything, their responses to the children's questions only serve to confound the children more and entrench the already present secrecy around their lives. For instance, when Odidi asks their parents who the books in the house belong to, 'Akai-ma had snarled, "Someone else's"' so Odidi takes to calling the mysterious Bolton 'Someone Else' (58). Akai's violent reaction to Odidi's question, by snarling, and her refusal to name Bolton enhances the element of ellipsis and therefore secrecy in the novel. The young Ajany's first encounter with the name of the mysterious man whose name is, for now, only a 'scrawl' (58) in books is presented in a stutter: 'H-U-G-H, Hugg Huff … Baba, what's a Hug-g B-Bolton?' (59). Ajany has no idea that Hugh Bolton is a human being hence the article 'a.' The question, in a faltering sentence not only indicates the child's innocence but also symbolises the obscurity around Bolton's name. Nyipir's is shocked at his daughter's question and his reaction, just like Akai's, betrays his unwillingness to discuss this issue:

> Nyipir's head had almost jumped out of his neck. In one move, he dropped the Bible, surged up, strode over, and snatched the book from Ajany's hands, snapping it shut. In a shredding tone he said, 'Brush your teeth. Go to sleep. It's late. You, too, Odidi.' (59)

It is as if naming, Bolton will bring back dark memories of the past for Akai and Nyipir and they almost hope that if Bolton remains unnamed then the past will not affect their present. They are afraid of the truth so they would prefer that the issue of Bolton remains silenced, hidden.

However, in the present, Ajany desires to understand her family but there is no one to answer her questions. Despite Odidi's death, Akai-ma's disappearance, and her father's silent grief, there is change but some things remain constant. Ajany tries to seek solace in the familiar but even then, her thoughts are disturbed and therefore cannot be expressed in a coherent manner:

> *What endures?*
> Heat of fresh milk.
> A kid butts Ajany's leg. She shoos it away.
> *What endures?*
> Galgalu.
> *What endures?*
> Fear of lunacy. …
> Nightfall endures.
> And when, later, flames sputter inside Galgalu's cracked hurricane lamp, an orange glow appears, the same as that which had assured two desert children that light confounds darkness. (60)

The repetition of the question 'what endures' indicates that in the midst of all the lunacy and unspoken secrets some things, like truth, remain solid which is symbolised by the concept of light confounding darkness. Odidi's death and Akai's madness are symbols of evil, destruction, and secrets but there is hope that the truth, if spoken, will free this family from the bondage of heavy secrets.

The arrival of Isaiah Bolton marks the beginning of the unravelling of the Oganda's secrets. Hugh Bolton's painting of Akai, which Isaiah brings with him, makes Ajany understand why Odidi 'had fled Wuoth Ogik's enchantment with silence. Silence would never why and how Akai Lokorijim, their mother, came to be the naked, potent, pregnant subject of Hugh Bolton's art' (70). As Ajany is trying to understand the confusing news about her mother's association with Bolton, Nyipir is trying his best to keep what he knows to himself; he is not willing to discuss Isaiah's father. The turmoil in their minds is narrated alongside the 2008 post-election violence. The tension in the country can only be captured in disjointed words, phrases, and sentences: '*Parties … eminent persons … bloodshed … peace … violence … Peace … spoken … honourable gentlemen … war … tribal politics …* ' (72). The elliptical statement echoes the violence in the country and also symbolises the destructive nature of war — words do not make sense in times of war. The present state of war allows Nyipir to reveal some of his memories of the past with Bolton but his responses to Ajany's repeated question about Bolton's identity betray his discomfort with reliving the memories of the past. His answers are incomplete and somewhat incoherent:

> We shared … *trouble.*
> The thing … Mau Mau …
> Ahhh! We bury evil with covenants of silence. … For the good of the country. … We know, nyara, that to name the unnameable is a curse. (72)

Nyipir's memories come back in snippets because he is afraid to remember and to tell Ajany the truth. He and Bolton had been involved in secret murders before independence and he has too many secrets which he dares not speak about, including his role in Bolton's death, but Isaiah's appearance in Wuoth Ogik confirms to him the 'death does not keep its secrets well' (73) meaning that the truth always has a way of emerging in spite of one's efforts to keep it covered.

Nyipir's past is intertwined with the history of the country. He alludes to the Mau Mau and the Second World War and the effects they had on Kenyans. His father and brother had disappeared in Burma during the Second World War and he was part of the forces fighting the Mau Mau back in Kenya. These are experiences he prefers to forget, to remain unspoken, but the present circumstances have forced him to 'retrieve rotten stories' (73), referring to things he would rather maintain silence about. Nyipir's desire to forget 'rotten stories' points to the post-colonial Kenya's constant timidity and unwillingness to actively confront historical injustices. Kenyans would rather be silent about the wrongs of the state because questioning such ills will cause pain. Ajany realises that they have been victims whose 'days were stuffed with chocked fear, suffocated by the family habit of silence' (82). She and her brother had always longed for the metaphoric 'daylight' (82) which refers to their desire to be free of secrets. Just like Nyipir's family is weighed down by secrets and silences, so is the country. The narrator insinuates that Kenyans have got to question their past, examine the ills of the ruling class, and fearlessly interrogate the unspoken if the country is going to progress.

One of the 'silences' that Kenya carries is the systemic marginalisation of Northern Kenya since the pre-independence period. The residents of Northern Kenya have no idea what goes on in the rest of the country which they refer to as 'Down-country' (71). When they talk about the 2008 post-election violence, they refer to it as if it happened in a foreign country which they have no connection with. They have to rely on an uninformed person for information about Kenya and they end up getting misinformed. Their exclusion from life in mainstream Kenya is captured through satire. Discussing the 2008 violence, the Trader, who is their main source of information, tells them that 'a man from Ghana named Choffeur had sent another, named Kofi Annan, to save Kenya. Kofi had in turn invited "Haninant Parsons." The trader goes further to claim that he knows "Chibaki", referring to [President] Mwai Kibaki, because "I sold him two camels, – no, no, three"' (89). The trader seems to think that 'Haninant Parsons' is one of the individuals, eminent persons, in the peace negotiation team led by Kofi Annan in 2008. Galgalu actually believes the Trader when he claims to have sold Kibaki some camels. The writer, through satire, mocks the pathetic situation where an entire region in the country is so far removed from the national narrative that the residents there exist as if they are not Kenyan citizens. In a way, their existence has been eclipsed from the national debate — there are ellipsis marks where their names ought to be on the national register.

The writer is concerned with the discourse of exclusion because it is what led to the post-election violence. That it is the uninformed Trader from Northern Kenya who tells the news of the appalling killings in Naivasha is an indictment of postcolonial Kenya about communities turning against one another so many years after independence. The Trader is expresses disgust at the violence by saying that the people who burned their neighbours in Naivasha 'watched [and] they ate food' (89). In other words, they were silent as a family was dying. The Trader refers to the situation as 'Godless news' (89) indicating that the violence was horrific and a major blot on the national fabric.

The news of the 2008 violence leads Nyipir to memories of the violence of the Mau Mau and the oaths of silence that members had to take to protect the secrets of their horrific deeds. The writer seems to suggest that independent Kenya need not experience violence since she already did during the struggle for independence. People died either for supporting or opposing the Mau Mau and therefore there is no excuse for violence today. As Nyipir confesses, 'Long ago, I carried Kenya's flag. It was not so heavy then' (90). What Nyipir means is that Kenya may be independent, but the nation's pains and burdens keep increasing over the years. The fragmented sentences indicate the weight that the nation carries today.

Ironically, Nyipir himself is a 'silence' in the nation because his records do not exist officially. Having been involved in gun-trading and cattle rustling activities in northern Kenya, he connives with the Trader to purge references to his life from all official records. His past as a trader in arms and stolen animals is part of the many secrets which he habours about his life. He is, therefore, doubly removed from the reality of postcolonial Kenya — as a resident of Northern Kenya and as a 'secret' citizen — a ghost. Nyipir the 'ghost' is a metaphor for many citizens who are only citizens on paper but do not receive their rightful services from the government.

The narrative of Selene and Hugh offers another level of ellipsis (silences and secrets) in the novel. Their relationship is intertwined with the history of the nation for the two had been part of the making of the Kenya colony. Selene's life is introduced in a flashback to 'two and a half years earlier' (95) which suddenly shifts the setting of the narrative from Wuoth Ogik in Northern Kenya to a hospice room in Sussex, England. Her introduction is cataphoric and she remains unnamed, only being referred to as 'the emaciated woman' (95), until the moment when she is ready to reveal part of the secret about her life with Bolton and their sojourn in Kenya. She is on her death bed and the narrator captures her ailing condition in short, fragmented sentences which indicate the weight of the secrets she has carried for so many years:

> Soft lights. Night obscured life's details. The emaciated woman limped around the bathroom of her hospice room in Sussex, easing a cramp in her right thigh. She used to be a marcher when she was not dying, when she was not seventy-eight years old. Touched her hair. Meager where it existed, once ink-black, worn page-boy style. She winced. Breathing was a chore. The cancer had spread. Curved spine. How tall was she now?
>
> Her nose twisted. 'I'm old.'
> Dying has a ghastly smell.
> She had been fragile until the visit.
> Her son.
> She had dreaded this, had hoped to avoid it.
> Now it had happened, adrenaline urgency.
> I love this dark. Not primeval, concealing, and heavy, like other darknesses. (95)

Selene is struggling to protect her son, Isaiah, from the truth about his father. She has kept the secret about his paternity for so many years that it is a 'heavy darkness.' Her mention of 'dark' and 'darkness' refers to the silence she has observed regarding Isaiah's father, but the time has come for her to reveal the truth. The metaphor of darkness is elliptical since it means that there is something hidden, covered, or shrouded in mystery. The burden of the secret is so heavy that she prefers the 'dark' of death to that of having to tell Isaiah the truth about Bolton, the man whose name she had 'erased' (96) and therefore dared not voice.

Selene realises that she cannot silence the truth for ever, so she decides to confess to Isaiah. She does so through a letter, an apt confessional strategy because, the letter form being a private mode of communication, it evokes a sense of honesty and a desire to break silences. Selene's letter tells Isaiah that the story he seeks to unravel is a 'dry well' (97) indicating an absence or a worthless venture. The statement foreshadows Isaiah's later realisation that, indeed, Bolton was not his father. Selene would not dare voice the truth that Isaiah's father was one of their servants; she would rather maintain the lie about Hugh being the father.

The various milestones in Hugh and Selene's relationship are narrated alongside the country's history. It is through the narration of their stay in Kenya that the narrator records important historical events in Kenya such as the 1952 visit by Princess Elizabeth and her ascension to the throne while in Kenya, the departure of Governor Mitchell, increased agitation for freedom by the Mau Mau, and the declaration of the State of Emergency. This was a period marked by great tension and fear — tension because of the war and fear, both of attacks by the Mau Mau and the fall of the colony. The narrator describes this tension and fear using fragmented sentences, a kind of ellipsis that only hints at the fear without giving detailed explanations:

> New favorite dinner topic: Mau Mau.
> Subtheme: kiapu — the oath, the covenant.
> Its dreadful mystery, the herald of shadows.
> Favorite rumor: insurrection.
> Favorite fear: death of the European.
> The unspoken: loss of a nation, nowhere else to go.
> The fear: requiem for an ideal.
> Selene thought: I told you so. …
> Mau Mau. Acrid fear. (105)

The settlers are uneasy about the imminent fall of the colony and are afraid of starting afresh. The above thoughts indicate their broken dreams about settling in Kenya and creating an ideal country. The disjointed sentences point at their feelings of loss — of time, money, and energy. For Hugh and Selene, the loss is bigger because it is that of a personal relationship — Selene wishes to leave but Hugh is determined to stay in Kenya.

Hugh is part of the colonial authorities that are keen to wipe out the Mau Mau. He does not reveal what they do at work and his words are few but loaded with silences and mystery: 'Pseudo-gangs. Economical. Effective. Population sweep. Flogging the Forest' (109). Selene desires the truth, but Hugh is more concerned about the 'unspoken' killing engagements that he is involved in as part of his service to the colonial government such as 'Hola — a work camp where an unnamed man goes berserk and pounds eleven inmates to pulp' (109). The killer is 'unnamed' which is a way of covering up for his evils. Hugh is transferred from Hola to Athi River but questions about this transfer are met with silence. Hugh comes through as a killer but his role in killing natives is kept as a secret.

Ajany's search for the truth about Odidi's death is a means to uncovering silences. Her search for Odidi is metaphoric of a nation's search for the truth, a desire to solve unresolved mysteries, break silences, and reveal secrets about the past. Her search points at the need for the nation to confront her dark past and deal with difficult memories. Ajany meets people who knew Odidi but are either unwilling or afraid to reveal what they know. One of Odidi's former colleagues cannot speak coherently and the ellipsis and hesitation in his words clearly indicate that he is holding back information: 'I'm Johinder. Uh, you know, uh … he left … maybe two years … maybe … ago. He … uh … hasn't, uhhh, called since … ' (168). Her conversation with Musali is quite brusque considering that he had been Odidi's best friend and definitely familiar with Ajany:

> 'Where's my brother?'
> 'Don't know, man.'
> 'Your friend?'
> 'Long ago.'
> 'What, friendship?'
> 'There was a deal.' (169)

Musali's curt responses betray his lies. He is keeping secrets about Odidi's life and he tries to cover this up by sounding casual and non-committal. The switch in the conversation from formal language to informal slang, even including sheng, is a way of trying to keep himself sober and steady as he lies to Ajany: 'Some stupid *jamas* tried to jack me. I was lucky. Cops *twanga-ed* them' (169). The truth is that Musali and his partners had betrayed Odidi when he refused to be part of a corrupt deal to fleece the country. He had also called the police when Odidi, later, came to him for financial help.

Odidi comes through as a fighter for the truth. Musali and his partners are sworn to secrecy about the corruption in the country, but Odidi refuses to be compromised and offers to resign. Musali and his partners vote Odidi out of the company to allow them a chance to partake of the corrupt deals and make money. In the conversation between Ajany and Musali, the word 'corruption' is not mentioned; the vice remains unnamed, yet it is part of what ails postcolonial Kenya. Musali justifies what they did and even attempts to scoff at Odidi for declining an opportunity to make money: 'This thing of mahonour ama patriotism, man — you must be practical. … Which Kenya did Odi grow up in? That *jama* could be so, so, so stupid, y'know?' (170–171). Musali is not only the face of Kenyans who stay silent about the effects of corruption on Kenya but also a symbol of greed. That he does not tell Ajany everything points to the guilt and shame he carries with him. He is a foil to Odidi who chooses to speak against corruption, who chooses voice over silence, and who the writer presents as a symbol of Kenyans who have been persecuted or killed for standing up for the truth — Pio, Mboya, JM Kariuki, and Ouko among others. Odidi's death is therefore symbolic of the silencing of the truth.

The writer indicates that one of the heaviest burdens Kenya carries today is the silence about, which consumes the nation. Ajany's search for Odidi, knowing too well that he is dead, is symbolic of Kenya's search for an honest national conversation on issues such as justice for the aggrieved masses. Odidi is persecuted for his efforts to raise the people's consciousness about the social and economic ills. He was 'crying out to citizens, trying to alert them to the reasons they were paying six times the price for bread, fuel, milk, and sugar. Why their shilling had plunged, and why there were now multibillionaires shopping for helicopters in their midst' (206). Odidi's concerns are those that affect Kenya today — inflation and the widening gap between the rich and the poor — but citizens have been boxed into silence. They dare not ask questions and they seem to be apathetic 'about why their lives [have] become harder' (206). Sometimes the truth is an illusion, a mirage, because of the culture of silence, but the writer is persuaded that the nation still needs to pursue that truth.

The writer indicates that the vice of corruption is not new and it has been present since independence. Nyipir had been part of the new post-independence administration that took it upon itself to carve out sections of the country for personal benefits. He was involved in state-sanctioned violence and displacement yet, ironically, was rewarded — for keeping state secrets. In the present, however, the memories of his past and the secrets he has had to keep constantly disturb him and he is so powerless that he can only say, repeatedly, that 'memories are ghosts' (131; 132). His thoughts about the past are presented in a staccato stream of consciousness which reveals his disturbed state of mind:

> He was in a platoon fanning out in the northern terrain, tracking scents. Women, children, and elderly equaled prey, equaled game. Blasting hapless homesteaders, AK-47-ing camel herds to encourage cooperation. They mowed down elephant families, loaded tusks into lorries with blacked-out number plates. Destination, Singapore via State House. The national economy of secrets. (132)

Nyipir covers up for a state that is destroying its citizens — treating them like animals (prey) and confiscating their livestock to force them into submission. By metonymically mentioning State House, the narrator intimates that the state is involved in poaching and therefore stripping the country of her natural resources. The 'blacking-out' number of plates is meant to hide the truth about the state's involvement in corruption. Just like the lorries' number plates are blacked-out so does Nyipir black out what he knows about the government's role in destroying the country.

The vice of corruption is also rampant among police officers. Petrus, for instance, questions Ali Dida about the possibility of a police officer who earns a 'simple' salary having millions of shillings in bank accounts and owning a 'simple' car dealership, twelve 'simple' butcheries, and three 'simple' lorries. Petrus claims that he is asking the questions that Kenyans do not ask, that is, about the existence of tremendously wealthy public officers who earn modest salaries. Through Petrus' question, the narrator indicates, sarcastically, that such people do not accumulate their wealth through hard work but by embezzling public funds and being paid to stay silent when the country is being destroyed. The repetition of the word 'simple' (271) is a sarcastic reference to the officers' supposed lifestyles yet they live lavishly at the expense of citizens. In addition, it is a strategy of provoking citizens to ask questions about corruption. The irony of the question is that Petrus is not questioning Ali Dida because he is concerned about the country. The truth is that Ali had blackmailed Nyipir into getting a share of the cattle rustling business and Petrus also blackmails Ali. Ali had traded the security of citizens by keeping silent about Nyipir's illegal activities and Petrus keeps silent about his discovery of Ali's corrupt transactions. The two of them are symbolic of the corruption in the police force.

Nyipir is being consumed by the many secrets he habours and the weight of his silence and that is why he finds it very difficult to speak to Isaiah. Isaiah's presence forces Nyipir to confront the ghosts of memories, which include the truth about Isaiah's father, which he would rather forget. The dialogue between them is characterised by ellipsis, fragmented sentences, and one-word responses (132–133) indicating Nyipir's unwillingness to reveal what he knows about Hugh. Isaiah is a man on a search and his unrelenting questions symbolise the need for the nation to constantly examine her past and question any hitherto unspoken topics. The memories provoke anger in Nyipir because facing one's past of wrong-doing is not an easy undertaking and neither is speaking about matters that one has kept silent about for a long time. His thoughts are presented in staccato form to show his disturbed state of mind because of being haunted by the ghost of memories:

> Yes. He knows the day, time, and emotion of the making of the painting. By the time he raises his head from the pit, a red-eyed meanness owns him. Rage. He has killed men before. He could kill again. (133)

Nyipir has killed not only Hugh but also members of the Mau Mau. These are some of the unnamed 'men' he refers to in his thoughts. He is so angry that he imagines that if he killed Isaiah then his secret would be safe.

Nyipir is not only haunted by the memories of his past but also experiencing pain and loss in the present. His son is dead, his daughter and wife have run away from home, his assistant Galgallu is missing. His sense of helplessness is summarised in a single word — 'absence' (215).

The gaps about the disappearance of Bolton in northern Kenya, and the investigation into the case, is narrated against the backdrop of the 1969 murder of Tom Mboya. The narrator recalls that citizens spoke to each other in 'whispers' and those who were associated with Mboya were 'silenced.' The words 'whispers' and 'silence' are used to show the fear that citizens experienced and the helpless state in which they found themselves since they could not openly question the murder of Mboya. They were forced into silence by the state and the murder remained unresolved. Similarly, the detectives find nothing but gaps as they try to locate Hugh Bolton. The Trader tells Ali Dida, the investigating officer, to ask Wuoth Ogik because 'a house like that — it would know about *wazungu*' (251). The Trader knows the truth about Bolton's disappearance, but his answer is elliptical because he does not want to reveal what he knows. He therefore only gives a hint by personifying the house (conferring it the ability to 'know') and erasing Bolton as an individual from the conversation and, instead, lumps him together in the plural '*wazungu*.'

The retrieval of Bolton's remains is communicated in an elliptical dialogue between Nyipir and Galgalu:

> Nyipir told Galgalu, 'There's something in the red cave.'
> 'It's forbidden.'
> 'For that reason, we go . . . .'
> 'It's time?'
> All the while, Galgalu had known. (283)

The incomplete sentences indicate information that is not being said. The word 'something' indicates a silence, something unspoken, while the 'cave' is symbolic of a secret. The narrator indicates that Galgalu had 'known' but whatever it is he had known remains unspoken.

The writer is convinced that the culture of silence in Kenya started with Mboya's murder in 1969. The constant allusion to this murder indicates the writer's persuasion that Mboya's murder set the country on a downward spin and citizens have never been able to ask questions about anything since then. David Goldsworthy reasons that Mboya was the man Kenya wanted to forget. Mboya's death in a way instigated the systemic death of the nation because 'after Mboya everything that could die in Kenya did' (1982, 285). The man alleged to have killed Mboya was hanged before he could reveal any secrets about 'the big man' (285). The narrator refers to the silence about the emptying of a people from Central province and the death or exile of those that did not make it out of the province and indicates that this information would not be in the public domain because of the 'oaths of profound silences' (285).

The writer decries the violent state of postcolonial Kenya by stating that after Mboya the country's official languages became English, Kiswahili, and Silence (286). No one dared ask about the men who had been 'erased' after Mboya. This is a suggestion of a culture of silence that characterises the country and which, the narrative implies, is part of what led to the 2008 violence. The intertribal tension that began in 1969 is carried in the memory of Kenyans and contributed to the violence.

The description of Presidents Kenyatta and Moi in the novel is prominently elliptical, symbolic of the nation's culture of silence. Mocking the folly of dictatorship, the narrator says,

> Later, despite a decree that had declared that it was not possible, somehow, the Leader of the Nation managed to die. In 1978, a lean cattleman, an inarticulate teacher, took

> charge, and Kenya changed again. Still, nobody dared talk about 1969 and why Tom Mboya died not even Nyipir. (288)

The words above indicate a kind of silence about the two leaders, as if nobody dares mention their names. The elliptical reference to them is symbolic of Kenyans' silence both out of fear of the two dictatorial leaders and their inability to voice their disgust with the ills committed during their era. The 'Leader of the nation' (Kenyatta) and the 'inarticulate teacher' (Moi) thus remain unnamed in consistency with the ills they represent. Moreover, the non-naming could also be a suggestion that these are the kind of men, unlike Mboya as Goldworthy (1982) suggests, who Kenyans should forget.

The various ills that have affected postcolonial Kenya have led to deaths — both physical and metaphorical — which the writer presents by creating a motif of death in the novel. Isaiah, talking about Wuoth Ogik, says, 'The house is dying' (297) which is a metaphor for the death of the individual, the family, and the nation. The individual dies either metaphorically of keeping secrets, as is the case of Nyipir and Ajany, or physically of asking questions as is the case of Odidi and Mboya. The family disintegrates because of secrets and dishonesty as happens to the Ogandas and the Boltons, while the nation dies gradually under the weight of fear and unspoken ills; the weight of whispers, to paraphrase Owuor.

The writer suggests that Kenya should accept a fourth official language — memory — because then the citizens would not be too quick to forget the transgressions committed against them. She indicates that memory would aid the country in returning to the beginning. As Nyipir says, it is important to 'go to the beginning. Even a lake keeps the memory of its mother, it is to her it strives to return, creating pathways that we follow' (306). The author seems to be saying that Kenyans need to return to the source of decay and death. It is only after confronting the ghosts of his past that Nyipir is able to talk to Isaiah and tell him about Hugh's death although he does not reveal his role in that death. Isaiah's search for his identity takes him to Kenya to unearth his parents' past, a form of returning to the beginning. Ajany goes to Nairobi on a journey to find out the real cause of her brother's death. Breaking silences, Owuor demonstrates, is not easy and the narrator demonstrates this difficulty through the elliptical conversation between Nyipir and Isaiah:

> What happened?
> Accident.
> What?
> His gun … went off.
> Where?
> Near here. *Here.*
> When?
> Before you were born.

How do you know this?
I … found him.

Isaiah has a semblance of closure because he has received some information about his [supposed] father but the fragmented responses, ellipsis and hesitation symbolise the unspoken truth that Nyipir is keeping away from Isaiah.

Conclusion

The writer's bigger concern appears to be that Kenya has been at war for a long time, but its citizens have acted 'blind and deaf' even when they saw the country being destroyed, 'for the sake of peace' (318). Yet, each Kenyan, by keeping quiet as the country disintegrates, could be accused of lacking a 'moral responsibility' and therefore being a 'little perpetrator' (3) of evil as Mark Sanders (2002) argues in *Complicities*.

The author appears to be saying that the ills committed by the state against its citizens have remained shrouded in secrets and silence. Some of these include the political assassinations, the murders after the 1982 coup, the 1984 Wagalla massacre, and the 1968–1989 'Kenyan interrogation' squad, a veiled reference to the infamous Special Branch of the police. The writer castigates Kenyans for 'memory loss' but is convinced that the silences will eventually be broken and the truth revealed. The beginning of Akai's 'madness' is revealed, Nyipir discovers that it is Akai who took away his animals, Isaiah gets to know the truth about his biological father, and Ajany discovers the truth about her brother's life just before he died. These revelations are symbolic of the end of silence and secrecy; the bridging of the gaps and ellipsis in the characters and the nation's lives. The characters' search for the truth is symbolic of the need for unravelling of secrets and silences that abide in postcolonial Kenya. The idea is that if gaps are bridged, silences broken, and ellipsis erased, then the land would begin to heal.

Nyipir, Akai and Galgalu leave Wuoth Ogik, a symbol of disintegration and a new beginning. Owuor demonstrates the rottenness of this society by showing Nyipir, as he is about to leave, the country, trying to gift Ajany with 'bank safety-deposit details … gemstones … [assuring her that] "it's all been arranged"' (380). Nyipir is trying to secure a financially stable future for his daughter using ill-gotten proceeds, which he claims to be money from 'trading' knowing too well that that's not true. The dishonesty behind his claim to trading is demonstrated by his hesitation when he is handing over the documents to Ajany: 'converted from money from … er … trading' (380). The author seems to suggest that regardless of the evils of the past, the nation can begin afresh; the ills can disintegrate to create room for a fresh start. When Nyipir realises that Ajany is not enthusiastic about his gift, he advises her: '… or leave it. Begin something new. Something that's yours. … You decide' (381). The pauses and truncation in their conversation suggest that beginning afresh is not easy, but it needs to be done.

Nyipir suggests that Ajany draws a picture of, among other things, forgiveness. Perhaps that is what the nation needs — to speak out and forgive the ills of the past. This way, the narrator seems to suggest, the nation can 'start again' (382). The novel ends with floods washing over the land, a symbol of cleansing and a new beginning. The elliptical reference to 'the woman' [who called out to] 'the man' without naming them, symbolises the coming together of a people who had previously been separated by silences and secrets. It suggests the healing of the land. The telling of the stories in the novel can be read as an invitation to participate in breaking silences, in filling in the ellipsis.

Disclosure Statement

No potential conflict of interest was reported by the author.

References

Bakhtin, M. 1981. *The Dialogic Imagination*. Austin: University of Texas Press.

Boehmer, E. 2005. *Colonial and Postcolonial Literature: Migrant Metaphors*. 2nd ed. New York: Oxford University Press.

Goldworthy, D. 1982. *Tom Mboya: The Man Kenya Wanted to Forget*. Nairobi: Heinemann.

Owuor, Y. A. 2006. "Weight of Whispers." Nairobi: Kwani Trust.

Owuor, Y. A. 2013. *Dust*. Nairobi: Kwani Trust.

Owuor, Y. A. 2019. *The Dragonfly Sea*. New York: Alfred Knopf.

Sanders, M. 2002. *Complicities: The Intellectual and Apartheid*. Pietermaritzburg: University of KwaZulu-Natal Press.

Soyinka, W. 2004. *Climate of Fear: The Quest for Dignity in a Dehumanized World*. New York: Random House.

Why and to Where Does Ajany Run? Culture and Femininity in Yvonne Owuor's *Dust*

Esther K. Mbithi and Julia Njeri Karumba

ABSTRACT

Launched around the time Kenya was marking fifty years of independence, Yvonne Owuor's *Dust* has been described as a 'cultural inheritance.' It portrays a collection of colourful characters who laugh at themselves in their search for some sense of belonging. This paper is a critical interrogation of how culture and gender shape the identities of characters in the creative works of East African writers. The present analysis focuses on the character of Ajany, in *Dust*. Ajany is a timid character who always lurked in Odidi's shadow. Initially she has no sense of self and seems to be on a journey in search of her identity. She makes international contact mentally, physically, philosophically, intellectually, psychologically as well as emotionally. Among what is affecting her self-realisation is the collective culture of her people and her gender. The study thus interrogates the contribution of femininity to the identity that Ajany eventually acquires. Since Ajany has interacted with different cultures in the search for self-realisation, the study also examines the effects of the different cultures on Ajany's character. The study is based on ideas of hybridity advanced by Homi K. Bhabha.

Introduction

Yvonne Adhiambo Owuor's *Dust* is about the Oganda family and the Kenyan nation. The setting of the opening scene is Nairobi during the hotly contested general election of December 2007 which escalated into violence that nearly tore the nation apart. The scene is indeed a vignette of violence in which a brilliant engineer turned criminal is gunned down by the police. Thereafter, readers are taken through a history of Kenya going back to colonial days and the emergency period; a string of seemingly unending eruptions of violence. This history is revealed through the upheavals of the lived experiences of Aggrey Nyipir Oganda and his family: wife, son and daughter. Nyipir, born near the shores of Lake Victoria, eventually makes a home in the drylands of Turkana in Northern Kenya, for reasons steeped in violence. The story of the Oganda family, like the story of the country Kenya, is the demystification of secrets from the dark past, in the hope of appeasing the future.

Running is at the core of the narratological structure of Owuor's *Dust*. Indeed, the story opens with a physical all-out sprint as Odidi runs for dear life.

> He leaps over two fire-painted blossoms resting on the stark cracked city pavement. (Owuor 2014, 7)
>
> ...
>
> *I want to go home*. Odidi lifts his feet higher, trying to fly. Odidi runs.
>
> ...
>
> Odidi runs.
>
> He turns down Jogoo Road and glances upward, childhood habit born when Galgalu, the family herdsman, had told him that God was *Akuj* — Eternity Revealed as Sky. (9)

Odidi is not the only character who does some running, though. There are many instances where we have other characters running: Ali Dida Hada, Petrus Keah, Akai-ma, Galgalu as well as Isaiah, who is a newcomer to the story, 'he had run and screamed and howled out a name' (264). In addition to the actual physical running, however, there is a great deal of metaphorical running throughout the text. Hugh Bolton and Selene ran away from England and came to Kenya (97). Akai-ma does a whole lot of running. Selene runs away from Hugh Bolton and Kenya just before independence, 'She had escaped from Kenya a few months before the December 12, 1963, Independence Day and returned to England. At Heathrow, she had almost fallen on the tarmac to weep for joy, delighted that at home death was wrapped in a decorous package, very genteel' (96). Indeed, Selene's letter to her son, written a lifetime later on her deathbed, hints at psychological running as well.

> *Darling Isaiah,*
>
> *There is a story behind every no, every maybe ... This is a story about a dry well. If you look — I pray you don't — you will find it close to a house of gargantuan pretensions, a pink folly. This is a small part of the man who dreamed it, built it, and offered it to me: Hugh Bolton. You've idolized him as your father. I fled his desert, left him with his gift, for I had found you, and for you I would have forsaken my life.* (97)

The psychological running (and hiding), effectively pervades the whole text. We take the character of Nyipir, Ajany's father, for example. As a young man, Nyipir hides from disappointment and murder: the disappearance of his father and brother; murders he has witnessed over time; murder he has prevented; murder he has committed: 'Nyipir spoke of an almost-teenage boy running from a psychotic uncle whose head he had split' (284).

Nyipir, the character who proudly carries the Kenyan flag in 1963, eventually goes into hiding from independent Kenya.

> To protect new post-independence citizen children, parents like [Nyipir] had painted illusions of a future Kenya, shouting out the words of the national anthem as if the volume alone would restore hopeful dreams. Keeping mouths, ears and eyes shut, parents had partitioned sorrow, purchased even more silence, and promised a 'better future.' (30)

Indeed, the character of Nyipir is a representation of the collective memory of Kenyans, who have been running away from, and trying to hide, the truth that is all around them: illiteracy, poverty and disease; made worse by tribalism, nepotism, and corruption. As far as running is concerned, physical, metaphorical and psychological, Arabel Ajany Oganda is the protagonist of this complicated story.

> Inside her room, numb. Weary of scrubbing tears away. She needs a destination. Maps made from her matter of memory. And that is when the walls start to close in. And she runs out of the room, out of the guest-house, out of the gates, into a darkening city. (174)

> Exhausted by mysteries, of confusing answers, fuzzy thoughts, bad dreams, drowning in unknown sensations, the accumulation of silences, Ajany rises up like a creature on fire and flies out of the room. She runs past Jos, onto the lawn and through the gate. (290)

Arabel Ajany runs back and forth, and round and round. Eventually she arrives, a lifetime later, at *Wuoth Ogik* (Journey's End), where she had started; a totally different person.

Literature Review

First published in 2013, *Dust* has been reviewed by many critics. One of the earliest reviewers, Ndivo (2014), predicted that the book, being well written and covering critical subject matter, would be 'widely read, researched and discussed.' In his review, however, Ndivo mentions Ajany in one sentence, as the sister of Odidi who '... maps her life from Wuoth Ogik to Brazil then back.' Gurnah's (2015) review in *The Guardian*, focuses on the metaphorical complexity that ties memory and stories to dust and flood. Mbithi's (2016) review does mention Ajany as a character to reckon with, in the sense that readers 'journey with [her and Isaiah] backwards and forwards in order to establish how they got to where they are as they are.'

As predicted by Ndivo, many research studies have been undertaken on the work. These studies, like the book reviews, tend to focus on the politics, history, landscapes, memories and emotional entanglements related to a tumultuous and violent past.

In her 2016 MA Thesis, for example, Liswaniso's interest is 'political violence', highlighting how 'different sections of the society are depicted as victims or perpetrators of political violence,' in a comparison between *Dust* and *The Uncertainty of Hope*. A different comparison, between *Dust* and *The Gift of Rain*, looks at 'postcolonial illuminations of past betrayals' (Gagiano, 2019).

Theoretical Framework

The arguments in this paper are based on the ideas advanced by Homi K. Bhabha (1990) on hybridity. Hybridity is, in simple terms, a mixture. In literary criticism, hybridity, which Bhabha also alludes to as the third space, refers to a position occupied when originals join to produce a new identification that is autonomous. According to Bhabha, the third space displaces the originals and opens up avenues for other positions to emerge. Even with this displacement, the third space retains traces of the originals that inform it. This means that hybridity, cannot in itself be original.

An interaction of different cultures results in cultural hybridity. This creates a totally new culture that Bhabha says is unrecognisable. A character yearning to belong to a culture that is different from what is considered the group or collective culture must forge forward in order to move away from that which dissatisfies to come up with a more fulfilling one. The new culture is consciously proud of the difference between it and the original one(s). This different new culture (a hybrid culture), however, retains some cultural aspects of the original(s).

A character who acquires a hybrid culture gains a hybrid identity and such a character occupies a space between the two cultures that have informed this hybrid culture. Stuart Hall argues that a shared or collective culture creates a true self that hides inside many other 'more superficial or artificially imposed "selves", which people with a shared history and ancestry hold in common' (Hall 1990, 223). Artificial oneness is not original; it is an assumed commonality that gives a character a sense of self.

Identity refers to a character's sense of self or sense of belonging. Jeffrey Weeks (1990) points out that identity is about belonging, what people have in common and what differentiates an individual from the others. This may include language, gender, history, ethnic group, or culture. If any of these aspects is shared among a group, then each member acquires a sense of belonging and contentment while in the group.

In a multi-ethnic state like Kenya, different ethnic communities have different cultural values and customs. Because of the different cultures, acceptance and appreciation of cultural diversity is a pre-requisite if there is to be peaceful coexistence among people of different ethnic groups. More often than not, there is a subconscious attraction between persons who have something in common: culture, for example. A people's culture encompasses language, beliefs, history and religion. Cultural oneness which arises from sharing these cultural aspects gives a character a sense of belonging. The character thus acquires a cultural identity.

As the work under study is authored by a female writer, this paper looks at the character under study, Ajany, through the perspective of feminist literary criticism. Though being female is biological and it cannot be reversed, femininity is a social construct. In many cultures women only become visible in the presence of their menfolk (fathers, husbands, and sons). The female character's sense of belonging, therefore, is attained while in the presence of the male character. There are, no doubt, women who take advantage of this and present themselves as being weak in order to rely on men, even in decision-making. By so doing, the female character loses her sense of self. This may be the reason female characters have been 'presented as being unoriginal, private and domestic — creative only in their biology' (Eagleton 1996, 7).

Our argument is in line with Freud's belief that people could be cured by 'making conscious their unconscious thoughts and motivations' (Freud 1949, 15). This would explain the eventual acceptance by Ajany of herself, her history and the power of choice within her.

Why Does Ajany Run?

Arabel Ajany, the second child of Nyipir and the fourth of Akai, was born under difficult circumstances. The pregnancy surprised Akai. The child, on delivery, was hot, and according to Akai-ma, she had refused to suckle. Her mother had left the unnamed child to die. On arriving home, Galgalu and Odidi, Ajany's elder brother, had asked for the baby. They had then set out to search for it. They had found the baby. Vultures were about to feast on her. They had saved her and Odidi gave her the name Ol Arabel after a river while Galgalu named her Arabel (a cool green mountain). To name something is to bring it to life (Owuor 2014, 35). Giving Ajany a name had thus driven Odidi to take full responsibility over her; he claimed that Ajany was his baby. From then on, Ajany had become Odidi's baby; to protect and to literally take care of. She had, therefore, learned to seek refuge in her brother. Giving Ajany a name is equivalent to giving her an identity. She thus acquires her sense of self through Odidi, her brother. As she grows up, however, Ajany is uncomfortable with herself. Perhaps even without realising it, she is in search of an identity, something she can proudly claim and hold on to. This may be the primary reason for her running. Ajany runs away from the unpleasant present, what Hélène Cixous (2005) refers to as 'the horror we would not live in the present' (xi), looking for a more accepting and comfortable space (identity).

Ajany runs away from the mother who has rejected her. Akai-ma had learned so late that she was expecting a child. When the baby was finally born, she was born hot (feverish). Akai had not named the baby because, according to her, those who are born hot die. Akai-ma was so afraid of losing the child that she chose not to have a relationship with her. Readers and the child do not know the mother's reasons until towards the end of the narration (Owuor 2014, 361–371). In the meantime, the girl child is traumatised and unsettled. Even after Ajany is given a name by Odidi, Akai never called her by her name. She always referred to Ajany as 'that one'. In the African cultural context, a person's name gives him/her a sense of belonging and therefore the character identifies with the culture of his/her people. Ajany wonders where she belongs in the mind of her mother. She asks in quite a sympathetic tone, 'And me ... where do I belong?' (37). Ajany's sense of belonging is only realised in the presence of Odidi. In Odidi's absence, she is lonely and 'takes refuge in stillness.' In running away, Ajany probably also runs from a fate similar to her mother's. She manages, unknowingly perhaps, to 'flee the fatal nail, the sword, the knife, the axe which threatens to fix, to nail, to immobilize [] in, by, death' (Cixous 2005, xi).

Ajany runs from her female school mates (other females). She seems uncomfortable in the company of her female school mates. They tease her into climbing a tree, then she falls down and hurts Odidi who had climbed up to help bring her down. Later, she bumps into one of those school mates in a supermarket. She spends as little time with her as possible, and even that little time is spent strategising on how to escape. The former school mate, in any case, is far more interested in getting an update on Odidi, Ajany's brother.

Ajany runs with her brother:

> They were chance offspring of northern-Kenya drylands. Growing up, Odidi and Ajany had been hemmed in by arid land geographies and essences. Freed from history, and the interference of Nairobi's government, they had marveled at Ka'alakol the desert lake that swallowed three rivers — the Omo, Turkwell, and Kerio. (10)

> He had started it, Odidi had. Their homelessness. He had conjured up stories of Elsewhere — imagined siblings, aunties, uncles, cousins, and grandparents, a web of doting dream relations into which he and Ajany inserted their longing to leave. (124)

Both Odidi and Ajany run from the shame of knowing that their mother had been pregnant before either of them was born (14). Growing up, no one tells them the truth, or the details of what happened, so they cringe in shame, and hide in the silence of 'not knowing.'

> Ajany and Odidi grew up surrounded by silences, memory and a solitary life brought about by lack of relatives (10). Odidi who seemed to have a solution for every problem that he and his sister Ajany had come across, had occupied the time narrating stories of relatives who never turned up. He told her of demons who were jealous of humans, Obarongo who was forever in search of little girls' eyes, and ogres who emerged from petrified silences. It was Odidi who told Ajany, 'we'll go Far Away'. (17)

There is a poignant scene (57) where Odidi tells Ajany to 'paint a river out of *Wuoth Ogik*' to take them to a new home. Both Odidi and Ajany run away from unexplained anger. Odidi is quite the academic. He finds books in a library and gets engrossed in them. When, with the natural curiosity of a child, he asks whose they are, he is told angrily 'someone else's' (58). He does not understand the anger, the attitude, much less the fear beneath the anger. Odidi and Ajany also run away from inherited guilt:

> Nyipir and Akai had planted new myths about *Wuoth Ogik*. It was an aborted mission base. Its disappointed priest had gone back to Europe, after giving over its stewardship

> to his assistant and friend, Nyipir. In Kenya's pre- and post-independence days, anything was believable. And a story repeated often enough became fact. (372)

In the end, Ajany runs from even her brother and from Kenya. She does not seem to fit in the culture of her people. She craves something different; something new. When she finds no sense of self in Kenya, she moves to Brazil where she hopes to find contentment. Whether she realises it or not, Ajany may be running in response to her feminine sixth sense; and it may be that the 'cowardly' act of running to Brazil is what ultimately saves her life.

Eventually, Ajany runs in search of her brother. Since Odidi had promised that he would take Ajany 'somewhere else', she swears to chase the absence resulting from his death until it takes her to 'Odidi's somewhere else'. This means that Ajany has been clinging to Odidi while he was alive, and in his death, she clings to his absence. His absence has, however, made her lose her sense of self. She comes to the realisation that she must go after Odidi's 'somewhere else' until she acquires her own identity. This means that she has to forge ahead to achieve a sense of belonging. Her desire to understand how her brother met his death takes her to Justina, Odidi's girlfriend who is pregnant (202). When they discuss Odidi, Ajany feels a little bit relieved. She feels that his rugby ball, which he had received at the university and which he always took with him, represents him. She embraces Odidi's ball as if she were embracing him. By so doing, she 'gathers her shattered selves by putting together pieces of Odidi' (197).

Arabel Ajany almost runs mad. The two instances cited above (174 and 290) are indicative of great psychological stress which forces Ajany to run. It seems as if it is therapeutic for her to summon all her energies into a physically straining exercise, in order to stop thinking. In running she releases the tension that is building up inside her mind. By the time her mother finally draws her into her arms for a hug, Ajany has begun to hear the sound of a child crying in her head. In fact, she asks her mother whether that is a sign of madness. To paraphrase Hélène Cixous [Ajany] had received blows from all directions right from birth, blows that have opened wounds, wounds which have 'translated into a haemorrhage of the soul' (ix).

To Where Does Ajany Run?

Perhaps without being consciously aware of it, Ajany is running away from the oppressive reality of the present. At a different level, she is therefore running away from the expectations of her culture and the society in as far as she is feminine. Failure to understand her roots had led Ajany to explore other ways of expressing herself and unleashing what was hurting her. She had turned to drawing. Her parents had reprimanded her when she brought home copies of her school paintings which had won the first prize in the national art show. What they did not know was that winning and being applauded in school had made Ajany feel contented in a school she hated.

Odidi encourages her to continue painting. Painting is the avenue that Ajany uses to express herself even after Odidi's death. Odidi has thus been a significant figure in Ajany's journey of realising her sense of identity. Ajany encounters a totally new culture in Brazil and she feels lost all the more. Since she has learned to fill the gap created by silences through painting, she continues painting the skull to fill the missing parts. This is the skull she and Odidi had found in the forbidden red cave; the cave of memory. History, which is a part of a people's culture, is represented by this skull. Ajany is also a sculptor, and as pointed out by Gurnah (2015) while talking about a different piece, Ajany's work is metaphorical, 'The metaphor is made concrete in the sculpture Ajany makes of her father's missing brother, whom she only knows from stories.'

Through painting, Ajany is fulfilling the promise she made to Odidi that she would keep painting. At the same time, the painting fills the void created by the cultural differences of her people back in Kenya and those in Brazil. This painting therefore makes her contented. Without realising it, her painting seems to represent therapy which releases her emotions, in Freudian terms, and eases her unconscious into the conscious. Running away, and painting, then, become Ajany's imaginative rediscovery, the avenue into a 'rediscovered essential identity' (Hall 1990, 224).

It is Ajany, home for Odidi's funeral after her exile in Brazil, to whom the parents confess; for whom they ask forgiveness; in whom they see a future. Nyipir speaks about his youth, his brother, his father, and his uncle (Owuor 2014, 284). He also talks about forgiveness (311). Akai-ma tells Ajany about her first pregnancy and the dead twins (361–371). She finally cries over the pain she suffered going through that pregnancy, being rejected, losing the twins in a drought and nearly being killed (362).

Ajany gains her sense of self in her father's presence and assurances. She describes Nyipir, her father, as standing where the outside world was separated from the inside melee. He thus occupies the gap between the others and her inner self that is not at peace. His presence at the airport when she arrives after Odidi's death makes her feel contented. The assurances of Nyipir when he calls Ajany 'nyathina' and pats her on the back calling her his own, make her feel secure. She thus feels contented.

As a girl, Ajany's timidity fades when Odidi takes her to the red cave; the cave of memory. They had been warned by their parents never to visit the cave. It was a forbidden place. She is told by Odidi to swear never to tell anyone that they had been to that cave. When she hesitates, he teases her that she is easily scared and therefore she must swear. Since she wants to prove to him that she is not silly, she swears and just as the soil she holds when swearing, 'something elemental inside her flowed away' (75). Her timidity fades and in its place, courage is born. She thus gains self-confidence and realises her sense of self through Odidi's coercion.

Interaction between different races breeds cultural hybridity. Ajany meets Isaiah Bolton after her return to Kenya from Brazil. Isaiah is a visiting Englishman who is searching for his father, Hugh Bolton. Isaiah had received a book from Odidi, bearing Hugh Bolton's signature and Odidi had thought the book would help Isaiah trace his father. When Isaiah comes and finds that Odidi has died, he is received by Ajany. Later, as Ajany moves to Nairobi to search for the cause of her brother's death, she meets with Isaiah, who has been advised to follow her for she may have answers to his questions. Ajany feels secure and warm in Isaiah's company. Their differences symbolised by their different skin colour, their different cultural backgrounds and nationalities, do not hinder them from giving each other a sense of belonging. The character of Ajany is quite different from many female characters in other works of art, especially in novels written by male writers, such as the character of Wanja in Ngũgĩ wa Thiong'o's *Petals of Blood* (1977).

Incidentally, as Ajany is calling Odidi on the phone from Brazil (Owuor 2014, 10), Odidi is being pursued by the police who have shot him after a foiled robbery. Ajany's calling and Odidi's dying are juxtaposed. Her confidence and trust in her brother are being replaced by his mortal absence. He therefore cannot answer her call. Since she had grown to be so dependent on Odidi, she calls repeatedly awaiting the kind of advice he would give since according to her, he had always known what to do and she trusted everything that he said. She has to sort out her own mess now. She later receives her father's call telling her to come home since Odidi is dead. Coming back home is a solution to her troubled self, since she is moving away from the crime she had just committed, of stabbing her boyfriend Bernado. Even though Odidi is dead, she would feel that she belongs in the place where she and her brother had grown up together.

In *Dust*, the character of Ajany has been carefully constructed. She starts life near death and grows up in the shadows — the timid, quiet sister of Odidi. She is presented as the complete contrast of her mother Akai-ma, who Kenny (2016) describes as 'at once fearless, unwomanly, and ungovernable' (3). By the end of the novel, however, Ajany has become a veritable force. Like her mother before her, she gets intimately involved with an Englishman. Ajany, however, does so on her own terms. The character of Ajany is, effectively, the feminist 'coup de grâce' of *Dust*, a postcolonial novel crafted by a female writer. In her research project, "Murder she wrote: Reading Yvonne Adhiambo Owuor's *Dust* as postcolonial feminist crime fiction," Mũrĩithi (2018) recognises this achievement and indeed considers Ajany as the 'postcolonial detective, a transnational figure suturing together, in her body and travels, Akai-ma and Justina, but also going where they cannot go in some instances' (11).

Eventually, Ajany's running is brought to an abrupt end by Odidi's death. When she receives news of her brother's death from her father, Ajany runs home. Her seven years in 'exile' have made her that much more confident. She has seen enough of the world to assert her presence. This change may be confirmation of what Rushton (2017, 45) says, 'Travel both within and away from the continent is a central part of Africa's global historical narrative.' Ajany comes to the realisation that it may be too late for Odidi, but she has been saved from his fate. After a tortuous journey around the world, she runs into self-acceptance and a hybrid identity.

> The territory of infinite pain.
>
> *Odidi.*
>
> She runs.
>
> Past Nyipir
>
> Arms flailing, feet gliding above the ground, she runs.
>
> Beguiled by her rush, the gathered gawk. By the time Nyipir kicks aside the gate to try to stop her, the darkness has already swallowed Ajany.
>
> Isaiah shakes his head to dislodge the lost-in-dreaming sensation that suffuses him.
>
> The trader stares into nothing with a finger across his face. 'It's out', he explains. 'Now it roams'.
>
> Silence. (Owuor 2014, 112)

Conclusion

Arabel Ajany runs a full circle. In the process, she undergoes a complete metamorphosis. It is at *Wuoth Ogik* (Journey's End) that Ajany's metaphorical wounds, which have been dripping since birth, find healing and finally dry up. In the final act of razing the coral house to the ground, Ajany finds closure. Having started out as an unwanted child, left by her own mother in the wild to die; having lived in the shadow of her brother for thirty-two years; she finally becomes the first-person universal, the survivor who has a future to look forward to.

Disclosure Statement

No potential conflict of interest was reported by the authors.

References

Bhabha, Homi K. 1990. "The Third Space: Interview with Homi Bhabha." In *Identity: Community, Culture, Difference*, edited by J. Rutherford, 207–221. London: Lawrence & Wishart Limited.

Cixous, Hélène. (Original work published 1998) 2005. *Stigmata*. London, New York: Routledge. doi:10.4324/9780203023662.

Eagleton, Mary. (1986) 1996. *Feminist Literary Theory*. Blackwell Publishing.

Freud, Sigmund. (1940) 1949. *An Outline of Psychoanalysis*. New York: W W Norton & Company Inc. https://www.google.com/search?q=psychoanalysis+by+sigmund+freud&oq=psychoanalysis&aqs=chrome.3.69i57j0l7.15022j0j7&sourceid=chrome&ie=UTF-8.

Gagiano, Annie. 2019. "Postcolonial Illuminations of Past Betrayals in Tan's *The Gift of Rain* and Owuor's *Dust*." *The Wenshan Review of Literature and Culture* 12 (2 June 2019): 1–27. http://wreview.org/attachments/article/324/Postcolonial%20Illuminations%20of%20Past%20Betrayals.pdf.

Gurnah, Abdulrazak. 2015. "*Dust* by Yvonne Adhiambo Owuor Review – A Complex Vision of Kenya." *The Guardian*, March 19. https://www.theguardian.com/books/2015/mar/19/dust-review-yvonne-adhiambo-owuor-kenya#:~:text=Dust%20by%20Yvonne%20Adhiambo%20Owuor,of%20Kenya%20%7C%20Books%20%7C%20The%20Guardian.

Hall, Stuart. 1990. "Cultural Identity and Diaspora". In *Identity: Community, Culture, Difference*, edited by J. Rutherford, 222–237. London: Lawrence & Wishart Limited.

Kenny, Christina. 2016. "She is Made of and Coloured by the Earth Itself: Motherhood and Nation in Yvonne Adhiambo Owuor's *Dust*." In *Africa: Moving the Boundaries Proceedings of the 39th African Studies Association of Australasia (AFSAAP) Annual Conference*, 5–7 December 2016, The University of Western Australia, June 2017. Accessed 14 June 2020. https://afsaap.org.au/assets/3-Christina-Kenny.pdf.

Liswaniso, C. M. 2016. "A Critical Exploration of Political Violence in Selected Literary Works: A Case of Tagwira's *The Uncertainty of Hope* and Owuor's *Dust*". Master of Arts Thesis, University of Namibia. http://repository.unam.edu.na/bitstream/handle/11070/1928/liswaniso_2016.pdf?sequence=1&isAllowed=y.

Mbithi, E. K. 2016. "Unsettling Dust, Fifty Years On." *SAUT Multi-Disciplinary Journal*. Also at www.creativewritingekm.com/unsettling-dust-fifty-years-on/.

Mũrĩithi, M. W. 2018. "Murder She Wrote: Reading Yvonne Adhiambo Owuor's *Dust* as Postcolonial Feminist Crime Fiction". Master of Arts Dissertation, University oof Pretoria. https://repository.up.ac.za/bitstream/handle/2263/72652/Muriithi_Murder_2018.pdf?sequence=1&isAllowed=y

Ndivo, Larry. 2014. "Engage: Discourses on Kenyan Literature". Accessed at www.larryndivo.blogspot.com/2014_03_01_archive.html.

Owuor, Yvonne A. 2014. *Dust*. London: Granta Books.

Rushton, Amy. 2017. "No Place Like Home: The Anxiety of Return in Taiye Selasi's *Ghana Must Go* and Yvonne Adhiambo Owuor's *Dust*". *Études Anglaise* 70 (1) 45–62. https://www.cairn.info/revue-etudes-anglaises-2017-1-page-45.htm?ref=doi&contenu=article doi:10.3917/etan.701.0045.

wa Thiong'o, Ngũgĩ. 1977. *Petals of Blood*. London: Heinemann – African Writers Series

Weeks, Jeffrey. 1990. "The Value of Difference." In *Identity: Community, Culture, Difference*, edited by J. Rutherford, 88–100. London: Lawrence & Wishart Limited.

Narrating Kenyan Silenced Histories through Fiction in Yvonne Owuor's *Dust*

Amos Burkeywo

ABSTRACT

The primary focus of this paper is to examine the intersection of history and fiction in Yvonne Owuor's novel *Dust* to unearth silenced (hi)stories in colonial and postcolonial Kenya while locating the text within its historical context. By examining intersection of history and fiction, the paper sees fiction as an effective device in reflecting and breaking Kenyan silenced socioeconomic and political stories. It postulates that through fictionalised history, creative writers create new insights to represent the past, as a way of recovering alternate histories that might have been stifled in the official historical account. Therefore, fictionalised history challenges the implicit closure present in the official version of history.

Introduction

The intersection of history and fiction allows writers not only to fictionalise history to capture history of a nation-state but also to narrate suppressed stories in a nation-state and break the silences in official history. Fictionalised history challenges the publicly prevailing and dominant notions about a nation and provokes conversations and engagement with the ignored 'other' facets of the nation's history. Therefore, fiction highlights historical realities which official history cannot evoke emotively and persuasively and creates a space for voicing the same realities. This paper, by reading the novel *Dust* discusses the nature of history and fiction as argued by scholars, makes a case for repressed stories and then examines the silenced stories in Kenya's history from the colonial to the postcolonial period such as violence, corruption, nationalism, and disillusionment.

Dust, a novel written by Yvonne Adhiambo Owuor, is a narrative set in Kenya from the colonial period during the anti-colonial Mau Mau revolt of the 1950s through to the 2007–2008 post-election violence. It revolves around the family of Nyipir Oganda (his wife Akai Lokorijom and their children Ajany and Moses Odidi Oganda), and the family of Hugh Bolton covering historical incidents in colonial and postcolonial Kenya. The narrative opens in 2008, amid the post-election violence that happened in the country, and shifts back and forth, from the past to the present, telling the story of Kenya as a nation characterised by violence, assassinations, corruption, succession politics, and disillusionment. In interconnecting 'key' and selected historical realities such as the Mau Mau rebellion, murder of prominent personalities such as Tom Mboya, Robert Ouko and J.M. Kariuki, and the 2007–2008 post-election violence with the stories of fictional characters such as Nyipir, Isaiah, Bolton, Odidi and Ali Dida Hada, *Dust* attempts to recall Kenyan history and to depict the silenced stories in a nation-state.

History and Fiction: Critical Issues

Kenya's history is the backdrop of the fictional stories in *Dust*. But how do the two subjects –history and fiction — intersect to present stories on the margin that have been silenced in the history of the country? Commenting on the historical novel as a source of history, Taylor (1938) argues that:

> History and literature are complementary, not merely in that, they are both testaments to man's growth through the centuries, but in that they are the products of a common vital urge on the part of human beings to explain those intangible forces of life, which, in the ultimate sense, become the most tangible of all motivations. (478)

Taylor's argument suggests that the close relationship between history and fiction shows one supplies the other with both source material and inspiration. Taylor further argues that the prime necessity of literature is imagination because literature is essential in reconstructing the past even though then history tries to shun imagination in the reconstruction of the past.

Whereas history attempts to describe past events as they *really* happened, if it can manage to do so, fiction depicts what can be considered 'true' from the point of view of the characters representing people at the time of the event. Therefore, fiction enables assessment of historical claims as well as a reconstruction of alternative historical versions, which often pass unrecorded in official history. Official history is, according to Martin Blumenson (1963), a subjective narrative, as it is usually told from the point of view of the powerful in a nation-state, while those on the margin have their stories repressed (153). Therefore, the lesser group, once suppressed, is forced to forget its histories. Hayden White (1987), in *The Content of the Form* also argues that official history depends upon the existence of a social centre that allows the historian to locate events in relation to one another and 'to charge them with ethical or moral significance' (11). White adds that the social centre makes it possible for the historical narrative to achieve closure as it neglects other narratives and annals.

The understanding White advances is that the historical narrative is informed by the historian's need to assert his or her authority over other competing versions of the past in order to privilege a historical narrative as only one of the discourses that attempt to truthfully represent the past. However, the paper argues that fiction plays a great role in narrating and interpreting historical realities of a particular time to reflect the silences present in the history of Kenya, such as stories of violence, assassination, corruption, disillusionment, despair and loss — and to give people on the margin a voice for their stories to be heard.

While narrating the history of Kenya, *Dust* gives alternative angles from which to reconstruct or recall the nation-state's past and margined stories or histories. For instance, *Dust* deals with the complex interconnections between fiction and history. The novel consists of a series of subplots centring on the intersection between personal, family and nation-state histories from colonial Kenya to 2008. It deliberately shuns the linearity preferred by official history, taking the reader back and forth within the nation-state to areas such as Nyanza, Fort Hall, Athi River, Turkana and Nairobi, mixing imagined situations and personal stories of Nyipir, Odidi, Akai, Ajany, Ali Dida, Petrus Keah and Hugh Bolton with historical events such as the Mau Mau rebellion against the British colonial government, independence celebrations, the assassination of Tom Mboya in 1969, the rise of Moi to the presidency in 1978, the 1998 bomb blast and the bloody post-election violence of 2007–2008. While creating these vast scenes, the text takes the reader through tumultuous Kenyan stories.

In discussing the stories in the text, I also recognise that the less powerful have histories to relate (to), that are silent in official history. Bethwell Ogot (2010) argues, 'We need a history that will not deny the evidence of oppression and corruption' (49). At independence, nationalist leaders attempted to create a national narrative that included all Kenyans, with the motive to ensure unity and development, but which actually ended up excluding other narratives that were equally important. Peter Simatei (2001) observes, 'The desire by nationalist leaders to construct a unified nation and originate an official history to rationalise and legitimise the sanctity of the nation precipitates the suppression of alternative histories and other possibilities of identity formation' (55). Since stories, especially those on the margin, were suppressed, Simatei points out that literature intervenes in the making of history by evoking the suppressed stories.

Due to the inadequacy of official history to address and provide a full account of reality, writers of fiction create alternative voices that challenge, add to and complement historical perspectives. In *Dust*, Owuor, makes a conscious effort to let characters such as Nyipir, Odidi, Ajany, Akai, Ali, Isaiah and the Trader, all on the margin of society, narrate their stories, thus giving their own versions of history, which in some ways contest the idea of a homogenous nation-state as portrayed by the official historical accounts. Despite the interconnectedness of fictional stories and historical events in *Dust,* the novel does not merely recall the history of Kenya; it also reflects the silenced socio-political realities for a period of more than 50 years from the perspective of alienated Kenyans.

In distinguishing narrative history and fictional narrative, Matt Oja (1988) argues that the history end of the spectrum is generally characterised by the big picture, the context as well as the events and both the social and an individual level. Oja argues that the writer focuses on the 'why' of events, as well as the 'what'. However, the fiction writer is engaged primarily in telling the story of 'what' happened and if he/she gives reasons, he/she does it on an individual and emotional level through the inner motivations of the characters, or the ways they are affected and influenced by external factors (119). In *Dust*, Owuor fictionalises the historical events in Kenya by drawing on the memory of fictive characters and their experiences that can be said to be ordinary and uses an omniscient narrator to foreground the stories, which are frequently ignored in official history. For instance, through Nyipir, the novel reveals the buried memories of colonial violence during the Mau Mau uprising against British colonial rule in the 1950s, and to the brutalities of the post-independence state. It also highlights political assassinations of Tom Mboya and J.M. Kariuki, politics of succession of Jomo Kenyatta, the 1982-attempted coup, multiparty politics, ethnic conflicts, the terror attack in 1998 and other incidences, like corruption.

Similarly, White (2005) notes that fiction is the repressed other of historical discourse and adds that the return of the repressed other (fiction) in history creates the simulacrum (the novel) that the history refuses to be (147). Through fiction, we experience the lives of Nyipir, Akai, Hugh and Selene during colonialism and later the lives of Nyipir, Akai, Odidi, Isaiah and Ali, among others, in postcolonial Kenya. Through the memories of Nyipir, *Dust* digs up memories of torture, violence, loss and hidden secrets that haunt Nyipir. The independent state, just like the colonial state, silenced the voices of ordinary people through violence.

Case for Repressed Stories

In studying multiple versions of narratives about the nationalist past of a village in India to identify the differences between postcolonial nationalist narratives of the villagers and the mainstream dominant elite story of nationalism, Badri Narayan (2007) argues, 'There is no single unified narrative about their remembrance of the national movement and the contributions of different castes in it.' According to Narayan, the nationalist narratives are mostly idealist, based on binary opposites of native versus colonial, and narrated with passion, hate and other emotional aspects (68). This suggestion runs counter to the perception by Eric Hobsbawm (1990) which suggests that a nation-state is a cohesive, holistic and unified unit because of the central government, one geographical boundary, one official language, a national anthem and one constitution (179). Such a notion is shattered when one considers that there are various multiple narratives contesting the state's official history at any one time. This could be because of the powerful and the less powerful having different perceptions of the past and present resulting from their different socio-political and economic experiences.

In any society, there is no homogenous unified history but many contesting and fragmented histories and multiple disparities because the nation is an imagined political community (Anderson 1983). In a once-colonised nation-state like Kenya, there exist different histories. Through fiction, Owuor counters the country's official history as a construct by the elite. The novel therefore emerges as a creative way of reconstructing or even deconstructing the official history. The fictional characters of the novel, in a way, visualise the past, which is drawn from their memory and imagination. Instead of making characters out of Kenya's history, Owuor creates fictional characters such as Nyipir, Ajany, Akai, Hugh Bolton and Ali who narrate their own stories; and, as readers, we read their versions of history and thus hear repressed stories within the nation. Through Nyipir, *Dust* reveals colonial atrocities against Africans in Fort Hall and after independence, as those who spoke out were silenced, while corruption and outlawed activities such as cattle rustling, poaching and trade in guns were the order of the day. Nyipir also experiences torture at the hands of the postcolonial government after Tom Mboya is assassinated. Odidi reveals the nature of corruption and police brutality in the present-day Kenya.

Colonial and Postcolonial Violence in the Nation-State

Matthew Carotennto and Brett Shadle (2012), writing on the question of colonial history and violence, argue, 'Twentieth century African history, and violence in postcolonial Africa, cannot be adequately understood until we better appreciate the history of violence. We do not lack in historians of Kenya's violent history' (4). In the history of Kenya, the Mau Mau insurgency against the British colonial administration led to a declaration of a state of emergency by the British between 1952 and 1959 to help control the supposed violation by Africans of the legitimised and privileged colonial space. Observing how fiction writers depict Kenya during this period, Simatei (2005) argues that 'Fictional representations of colonial violence in Kenya demonstrate complex linkages between colonial violence, the violent responses to it or decolonisation, and the violations of the rights of citizens in the postcolonial/neo-colonial state' (85). Colonial administrators had employed force to appropriate African land, imposed tax and turned Africans into wage labourers, and even sent thousands of young African men to their deaths as guards during World War I and II. When Africans retaliated, after suffering for long, the administrators used violence to not only conquer the Mau Mau fighters, but physically and psychologically crush civilians and fighters in detention camps as well.

Owuor, in depicting violence through *Dust*, interrogates the tragic incidents of violence perpetuated in colonial and independent Kenya. Violence reveals the underlying conflicts in a society and manifested through use of force on individuals, groups or nations. It is meant to cause physical or emotional harm and sometimes leads to death. The novel constructs a narrative in which violence started during the colonial period and persisted after independence and haunts the nation-state. During the colonial period, colonial officers abused and tortured Africans and engaged in rule by fear, especially during the counter-insurgency campaign against the Mau Mau. Some arrested Mau Mau fighters were castrated in detention centres, forced to suffer hard labour, or beaten to death.

Bolton was part of the settlers who desired that Britain should maintain its Kenya colony under all means. He was determined to remain in Kenya by exerting power saying, '*Power is useless if it cannot be expressed*' (author's emphasis) (Owuor 2014, 101). Through Bolton, we learn how the colonial masters mis-treated their African servants. Bolton would always refer to Nyipir as *mtu shenzi* (bastard). After Akai became pregnant, he refused to marry her, condemned her as a prostitute, chased her away and almost killed her when she returned. By articulating the story of Nyipir, interwoven with histories of the Mau Mau struggle, Owuor helps to pinpoint colonial-sponsored violence from the perspec-tive of an ordinary person.

Africans were arrested, tortured and some hanged, and their bodies dumped in valleys. While at Fort Hall, at the peak of the Mau Mau revolt, Nyipir encounters gross human violation by the colonial regime. He meets Warui, the gravedigger, who buried bodies of Africans killed. Nyipir joins Warui in burying the bodies to make some money, but the narrator says Nyipir had not yet understood that the interrogating units were killing many people and it was difficult for Warui to bury them. The narrator also captures the trauma that Nyipir experienced throughout the Mau Mau rebellion. While at the British police camp, the commandant orders Nyipir to join a group of men sent to retrieve bodies from a hut, he encounters a beheaded old man, a hanged youth, a toddler and two split bodies of young women. Nyipir also sees Aloys Kamau, a catechist and a teacher of children, dead (170–171).

Whereas official history narrates the heroic efforts of the Mau Mau to liberate the nation and notes individuals like Dedan Kimathi and General China as those who fought to liberate the nation-state from colonialism, stories surrounding those who were tortured to death and those who witnessed and experienced these atrocities are only partially told. The official state history fails to grasp and negotiate several and mysterious experiences of the Mau Mau wars and struggle for freedom and the trauma after independence. *Dust* reflects the failure of official history, through exclusion of ordinary people's traumatic experi-ences as represented by Nyipir during the Mau Mau rebellion.

The state-authored official history produces an exclusive linear narrative that seeks to repress stories on the margin of a nation-state, yet within the nation-state are ordinary people's stories that haunt it. Postcolonial Kenya was no better than colonial Kenya. After Kenya attained independence, citizens expected that the new government would end torture and suppression that had character-ised the colonial government. But detention and imprisonment continued as individuals seen to be opposed to the postcolonial government policies were arrested, tortured or assassinated. The narrator says that after independence, fear split words into smaller and smaller fragments until words became secret and suffocation came. The state was seizing people, and no one cried. Reflecting on Kenya, Nyipir tells Ajany that Kenyans had been at war before she was born and the nature of war has been its silence because of not having resolved conflicts and challenges such as corruption, assassination and unfulfilled promises after independence. Nyipir remembers how bodies started showing up mutilated and dead and the loudest protests were created out of whispers (25).

At independence, the ruling elite fashioned a national identity to hold Kenya together by creating national myths based on selective memory and amnesia to create an effective governing ideology. The national myths such as we are one united country; we all fought for independence, found in state-authored history and the Constitution and propagated through government apparatus, were political devices to provide authority and legitimacy for the ruling political elite. These ruling elite repressed memories of the colonial past that threatened the call for peace, love and unity in independent Kenya. Marshall S. Clough (2003) avers that remembering the 1950s in Kenya means not just evoking the Mau Mau cause and struggle; it also means remembering the emergency, the killings and executions, the repression that evoked pain and ambivalence (254). Clough adds that when Kenyatta took over, he ensured continuity of the previous political regime's ideologies. To ensure that people forgot about the Mau Mau, the government followed the policy of amnesia towards Mau Mau memory.

He further observes that the policy of amnesia was encapsulated in the official slogan of 'forgive and forget', in that remembering led to division and forgetting led to unity (256). The elite appealed to the masses to embrace forgiveness and reconciliation while turning coercive power of the nation-state against those who refused to surrender their discordant memories. The citizens were silenced for the sake of peace and those that spoke were branded the enemy of the nation-state. The narrator notes, '*From now on, we shall not speak of so-and-so again. Anybody who mentions this name is an enemy of our nation*. Afterward, nobody was even willing to admit that so-and-so had even existed' (302; author's emphasis).

The police service is charged with the responsibility of maintaining law and order in a nation-state. However, an examination of the behaviour and operations of the Kenya Police, as depicted in *Dust*, reveals it has always been unscrupulous in dealing with the public and suspected criminals. One of the incidents that Owuor uses to depict police brutality is the killing of Odidi. Although Odidi is a suspected criminal, he is shot to death instead of being arrested and charged in a court of law. The police strapped a pistol to his chest and claimed that his gang had stolen one million shillings from a bank, yet the Officer Commanding Police Division (OCPD) had been hiring a gun to Odidi's group in return for a monthly fee.

Ajany meets an angry mob in a Nairobi City suburb staring at a man shot in the head by the police for impersonating a police officer. When Ajany wonders why the suspect was executed instead of following the legal procedures of handling the case, Assistant Commissioner of Police, Petrus Keah tells her that the police always have a thousand reasons to implicate a person, adding that if Ajany has any evidence, she can present it to the police. According to Petrus, every crime story begins with a decision and finally execution and that the police always have a reason, 'Maybe he attacked our officers. Maybe he was resisting arrest. Maybe he was a mad dog. A terrorist. Maybe he was planning a raid. We have a million reasons nyar Oganda. And we can apply these to you too' (194). When she asks Petrus about Odidi, Petrus tells her to go home, as no truth will set her free.

The government also uses the police to silence its critics. After the death of Tom Mboya, Nyipir undergoes torture at the hands of the police for speaking out. The Trader reveals that Petrus was part of the Kenya interrogation squad from 1968 to 1989. Part of Petrus' works included interrogating Nyipir. Petrus was also involved in the Wagalla Massacre in 1984 as 'He had overseen the washing of blood-spattered Wagalla runway, had arranged burials in secret sites, had terrorised would-be witnesses into what should have been eternal silences' (323). Owuor finds it apt to re-live the Wagalla Massacre experience for Kenyans to remind them to talk about other massacres such as Bulla Karatasi in 1984, Malka Mari in 1981 and Lotiriri in 1984, massacres in which hundreds of civilians were killed and the nation-state security agents committed other atrocities such as torture, brutal beatings, rape and sexual violence. The Wagalla Massacre was a result of a campaign by the government of Kenya to disarm the Somali Degodia clan in a town centre near Wajir in February 1984. The government reported that only 57 people were killed but according to the survivors, close to 5000 people died. After the incident, the atrocities were muted in Kenya's history until the Truth, Justice and Reconciliation Commission (TJRC) heard testimonies from people who witnessed the massacre carried out in a country by its own soldiers. The TJRC (2013) states in its report that 'close to a thousand' people were killed in Wagalla but it was unable to determine the exact number of persons massacred.

Narrating Corruption

In postcolonial Africa, political regimes have been associated with grand corruption that has favoured the political leaders and elites. Osoba (1996) refers to the term corruption as:

> A form of antisocial behaviour by an individual or social group which confers unjust or fraudulent benefits on its perpetrators, is inconsistent with the established legal norms and prevailing moral ethos of the land and is likely to subvert or diminish the capacity of the legitimate authorities to provide fully for the material and spiritual well-being of all members of society in a just and equitable manner. (372)

Owuor depicts corruption in Kenya at individual, business and political levels. According to her, corruption has been happening since independence and has become the norm. While the postcolonial regime silenced critics and repressed memories under the guise of national identity, ethnic and regional elites in power enriched themselves through corruption at the expense of the poor. The narrator says that immediately after independence, a new word came about, '*nyakua*', meaning grab, but it was cleansed to mean hard work. The 'hard work' involved taking over resources such as land that the colonialists had left (Owuor 2014, 25–26).

Through Ajany's initiative to unearth the circumstances behind Odidi's murder, Owuor explores how levels of corruption have to some extent overwhelmed social justice among Kenyans. Odidi had refused to take an oath to silt the dam that provided electricity to the nation-state so that the company could earn 30% profit for 10 years. For Odidi, this amounted to impoverishing Kenyans. Revealing how Odidi died, Petrus says Odidi was foolish in that if he wanted money, he should have joined politics. Petrus thinks that the desire for money pushed Odidi into robbery, but the truth is that Odidi became impoverished after he was thrown out of his own firm and his mortgage withdrawn after opposing a corrupt deal.

The narrator tells us about scandals that have occurred in postcolonial Kenya, including the Goldenberg and Anglo-Leasing scandals. Whenever a scandal is unearthed, the government forms commissions of inquiry to investigate the suspects but the culprits are never charged. What follows are dragged out court battles until the cases are withdrawn. A good example is the Goldenberg scandal in which Kenya lost Sh158.3 billion. After protracted court battles, the High Court dropped all Goldenberg cases in May 2013 because none of the cases presented had been concluded in almost two decades. In the ruling, the judge issued an order prohibiting the State from instituting any further criminal proceedings against the suspects (Lucheli 2013, 6). In the Anglo-Leasing scandal, billions of taxpayers' money was lost through payments based on promissory notes allegedly processed in return for fictitious projects that could not be verified. The persons responsible for the scandal are still at large. This has been a habit since independence as those involved in corruption scandals are left to go scot-free while the government and the people of Kenya continue to lose money.

The way the Kenya police service is administered suggests it is a warped institution. Ali, the Assistant Commissioner of Police, while on an investigation mission in the north of the country, joins Nyipir in the outlawed trade of smuggling contraband goods and cattle rustling. He could warn Nyipir of an impending attack, misdirect government informers, and restructure messages dispatched from the police headquarters (Owuor 2014, 261). Whenever a police officer is caught in a corruption incident, he is sent to Northern Kenya as a form of punishment. Such is the case of Aaron Chache who, while working as a traffic police commander along the Nakuru Naivasha highway, is transferred to Northern Kenya when he and his colleagues are caught by anti-corruption police officers receiving bribes (207).

Owuor taking on corruption through fiction illustrates the extent to which the country has 'normalised' the vice. Kenyans have accepted taking and receiving of bribes as a way of life. The financial scandals involving the government and individuals, private or fictitious companies are never regarded as a national debacle. The government that is supposed to deter corruption is at the heart of propagating it. Once it forms a commission of inquiry, there are hearings and then the reports are shelved and soon another financial scandal is in the offing. Within the government are colluders that are always scheming ways to reap from the country's coffers as they collaborate with the state officials. Political elites hamper the fight against corruption, as they are keener to shield one of their own from prosecution. The apparatus such as the police too have embraced corruption as a way of benefitting themselves. When individuals, such as Odidi, rise up for the good of the country, even civil society organisations and the media, who seem to advocate good governance, shun him. The citizens too are ignorant of the vice, yet they incur the expenses that result from corruption.

Nationalism and Disillusionment

The history of Kenya is punctuated with snippets of nationalism and disillusionment. Scholarly evidence show that several individuals played different roles in the fight for Kenya's independence from the onset of colonial rule. But after independence, the political leaders and elite that that took over from the British had promised Kenyans a great country of peace, love, unity and equity in sharing resources and opportunities. The masses had dreamt of a Kenya where everyone was guaranteed all their needs would be met and they would not be discriminated against. But postcolonial Kenya turned out to be another colony presided over by African elites.

Jude Agho (1993) observes that post-independent Kenya, like many other countries in Africa, is faced with another rift: a horizontal rift dividing the elite from the mass of the people (121). Agho adds that contemporary Kenya has not only witnessed the frustration of the peasants who had hoped for a better life after independence, but also deepening impoverishment and exploitation. Hardly had the citizens enjoyed the fruits of independence than the government started to unleash violence on those who voiced their opinions on corruption and misuse of power. The national myth that the ruling elite created in Kenya required coercion and sometimes even brutality to wipe out contradictory memories that questioned the 'truth' of the officially endorsed history of the colonial past.

The African leaders assumed the powers of the colonialists, misused power for selfish gains and shunned the spirit of nationalism. After his release from prison, Kenyatta refused to recognise Mau Mau achievements, criminalised the movement and condemned it as a 'disease' that needed the strong medicine of hard work and honesty to cure (Ogot 2010, 11). Individuals who were dissatisfied with the government's capitalistic policies that favoured the ruling elite, while the poor continued to suffer, were profiled as rebels, imprisoned and tortured. The

Mau Mau fighters who had fought for the return of alienated land continued to languish in poverty as leaders plundered the resources and consolidated their political power.

Owuor attempts to evoke national consciousness over the issue of nationalism and nationhood in Kenya. During Independence Day celebrations, the narrator says that as Nyipir marched, there were

> Men on podium, some who he thought had died. Two men he knew had pounded other men to death. Another had been detained for his own safety and been supplied with a stream of world literature and unlovely comfort women, one of whom he married. He had focused on one man — Tom Joseph Mboya … years before scoured the landscape and found promising souls that he sent to America … (Owuor 2014, 25)

One striking incident here is that of the detained fellow who was supplied with world literature and had a comfort of women, and he was now part of the leadership. Perhaps what Owuor attempts to depict in this scene is that some individuals benefited more than the Mau Mau freedom fighters concerning the fight for independence and those were the 'real' nationalists.

Kenyans, under the spirit of patriotism, fought for freedom and after obtaining independence under the 'invented' nation of Kenya, they felt a sense of belonging. Nevertheless, it soon emerged there were 'genuine' individuals in independent Kenya who deserved to eat the fruits of independence. Odhiambo and Lonsdale (2003) note the 'Kenya's arguments about its freedom's divisive birth, about who sacrificed most to bring freedom, about whose contributions has been most unjustly forgotten, or whose has most selfishly eaten the fruits of independence, and at whose expense' (2). By describing the independence celebrations scene, Owuor asks the question: Who participated in the birth of the nation-state of Kenya and who should eat the fruits of independence? Ogot argues that there has always been an attempt at imposing an official interpretation of the Kenyan past by selecting one identity. The government set up a National Taskforce to seek the views of Kenyans on who should be considered heroes and heroines of the nation-state and yet the same government had already identified nationalists to be recognised as national heroes, including Dedan Kimathi, Bildad Kagia, Paul Ngei and Koitalel arap Samoei (Ogot 2010, 28–29).

The question that lingers is what the place of ordinary people is, who, in their own way, contributed towards national liberation? What about the Mau Mau fighters who sacrificed their lives in the independence struggle? What about individuals like Odidi who, since independence, are still patriotic enough to fight corruption? Sadly, Odidi's steadfastness does not follow the script of the official history of postcolonial Kenya. He joins the ilk of 'insignificant' Kenyans devoted to fight bad governance, but he is never honoured. Parents such as Nyipir, seeing Kenyans who criticised corruption and misrule suppressed, experience the illusion of a 'future Kenya'. Their mouths, ears and eyes were shut, and they partitioned sorrow, purchased more silence and waited for better 'Kenya', which never turned up (Owuor 2014, 10). Nyipir had warned Odidi against meddling in the affairs of the nation-state (10). After Odidi was fired from Tich Lich Engineering Company, which he had founded with his friend, he went to the streets to petition people to stand up against corruption and injustices that had become a norm in society. With no means to survive and his mortgage recalled, Odidi is disillusioned and becomes a criminal. Odidi died in what Ajany says came from heroic idealism as he had been organising the disenchanted youth to work for a different future for themselves and it was sad that the 'stupid' nation-state did not have the capacity to grasp Odidi's vision and instead destroyed him (287). By recounting the story of Odidi, Owuor narrates the disillusionment and despair that have characterised Kenyan since independence. Odidi's story is a representation of the stories of individuals in Kenya who, after futile attempts to secure a nation-state free from corruption, end up with despair in their bowls. They resort to crime, die poor or are killed by the nation-state for criticising its dire leadership.

In an ideal nation-state, Odidi and individuals of his ilk would have been regarded as heroes but the official history does not recognise such individuals. According to Ogot (2010), the official history that we have is a glorious one that denies the evidence of oppression and corruption (48–49). It does not explain why, almost five decades later, Kenyans are still disillusioned, why corruption is still rife and why we have not realised unity despite calls for it since independence. Ogot argues that as a nation-state, we require a history that seeks to explain, '... why the high hopes associated with the struggle for independence have been disappointed, and why the legacy of nationalism in Kenya has not resulted into a cohesive society ... ' (50).

Political Assassinations

One of the key assassinations in Kenya, and which Owuor dwells on, is that of Tom Mboya who was minister for Economic Planning and Development in the Kenyatta government. Parselelo Kantai (*Daily Nation*, 2009) writing about Mboya 40 years after his assassination, attempts to unravel the reason behind Mboya's murder. Kantai says that the sense of optimism that had come with independence and somehow survived the ideological discord within KANU was extinguished with the assassination of Tom Mboya. After Mboya's death, Kenya became a nation of cynicism. Suspected assassin, Nahashon Isaac Njenga Njoroge, while being sentenced had asked, 'Why pick me? Why not the big man?' This clearly points out that there were other people involved in the assassination. Since then, fingers have silently pointed at individuals within Kenyatta's inner circle.

Charles Hornsby (2012) notes that Kenyatta's closest allies, facing revolt amongst the Luo and horrified by Mboya's murder, reverted to their ethnic bailiwicks. Delegations of Kikuyu and later of some Embu, Meru and Kamba were taken in their thousands to Kenyatta's house in Gatundu to take 'tea with Mzee' and to swear oaths to keep the presidency in the 'house of Mumbi' as a way of paying allegiance to President Kenyatta. Although there have been speculations over the murder of Tom Mboya, scholars and historians have failed to exactly pinpoint who was behind Mboya's killing. According to Kantai, Mboya's death caused the most severe riots in post-independence Kenya's history and had deepened existing ethnic and political divisions to the point that they threatened to break the country apart.

Owuor puts stories of assassinations into perspective when she depicts how ordinary people received the news of Mboya's death, especially those who felt heartbroken. No one could talk about atrocious incidents like assassinations as the government would arrest and torture them. It is unimaginable that even after the assassination of Tom Mboya, Kenya went on with the rhetoric of a united country, as members of the ruling party pledged undying unity to the president while the masses were expected to keep quiet about it. However, Mboya's death was so heart-wrenching that ordinary Kenyans could not keep calm. When Nyipir heard about Mboya's death, his body temperature dropped, his heart slowed down, and he shivered (Owuor 2014, 272). This seemed like Kenya had been killed and, therefore, dreams were shattered.

To express the silenced memory, fiction becomes a means to search for an experienced past, to reveal the past atrocities and trauma. Memory thus plays a key role in recollecting the atrocities that Kenyans experienced during the colonial and postcolonial period. Ogot notes,

> If memory is kept alive in order to kindle and cultivate old hatreds and resentment, then it is likely to culminate in vengeance. However, if memory is kept alive in order to transcend hateful emotions, to free oneself or one's society from the burden of hatred, then remembering has the power to heal. (2010, 194–195)

Nyipir, having worked as a police officer, is able to narrate the events he experienced. Reflectively, he tells his daughter that after Tom Mboya died, Kenya's official languages became three: English, Kiswahili and Silence. However, because there was silence, he tried to memorise some of these events. The narrator says, 'The core of post-Tom Mboya Kenya had been cracked. Nothing was certain, not even hope. Citizens spoke to one another in whispers … When those associated with Tom Mboya and his name were hunted down like vermin, there was silence' (Owuor 2014, 234).

In the aftermath of Mboya's assassination, most of the witnesses died while those who dared to speak were arrested, prosecuted and killed (273). People were prosecuted and sentenced at night. Those that were guilty were loaded onto the back of a lorry and corpses would be found heaped in large holes dug on appropriated farms. Nyipir was among the many individuals who were tortured. Three days after he was discharged from the police service, Nyipir was summoned to the headquarters where his colleagues tortured him. They held him and examined his teeth as if he was a cow, shaved his moustache with a razor blade and beat him. The narrator says that a trail of bowel-loosened muck stained his trouser and the floor. The torture that Nyipir underwent suggests alternative experiences and recollections of Mboya's assassination and other assassinations in Kenya's history. These incidents seemed dangerous to the country and had to be repressed. Nevertheless, the state's attempts to control how people recollect the experiences failed partly because it is difficult to erase a memory.

What should be noted is that the suppression of memories of the assassinations, torture and corruption incidents contributed to and continued the authoritarian leadership in Kenya since independence. Apart from Mboya's assassination, the cause of other killings such as that of Pio Gama Pinto, J.M. Kariuki and Robert Ouko have never been unravelled although there have been various investigations. The government, to some extent, has been put at the centre of responsibility for the assassinations but it has always denied this, with distorted evidence leads and the silencing of those who could testify against it. Having observed assassinations since the colonial period, Nyipir says dying began a long time before the deaths of Pinto, Mboya, and J.M. Kariuki. The assassinations of Pio Gama Pinto, Tom Mboya, and J. M. Kariuki are attributed to the state terror machine during Kenyatta's regime. Either very powerful people in the government committed the murders or extremely influential people outside the government, as a scheme to scare individuals inside and out of the government perceived to be opposing the regime, to remain loyal to the government, were responsible.

Election Violence

The 2007/2008-election violence that ripped the country demystified the notion that Kenya is a united and peace-loving country. The announcement that Mwai Kibaki, the Party of National Unity (PNU) candidate had won the presidential vote sparked ethnic conflicts that led to violence in which more than 1500 were killed. Supporters of Raila Odinga, the Orange Democratic Movement (ODM) presidential candidate took to the streets to protest what they believed were fraudulent elections (Opondo 2014). Moreover, by many accounts, the election had not been free and fair. Keith Somerville (2009) observes that violence has been rife in Kenya since independence. Politicians, desperate to protect their power or to challenge the powers of local or national rivals, employ violence to maintain their own power bases and to incite violence against their opponents. As for the 2007 elections, Somerville (2009) notes that there was violence during the latter stages of the campaign, but it escalated following the announcement of the results and accusations by the losing candidate, Raila, that the count in the presidential election had been a sham. The violence that followed was a result of the frustration of those who felt they had been cheated of victory, combined with extensive organisation by political elites fearful of losing — or not gaining — power or patronage (538).

Owuor attempts to paint grim scenarios of the 2007–2008 post-election violence to remind us of the recent history that we can otherwise easily forget. Once the coalition government was established after the disputed elections, Kenyans began chanting songs of unity calling for 'let us forgive and forget.' She explores the election violence, although from the perspective of the characters on the margin of the society. After the elections, the narrator tells us how Nyipir and Ajany followed the news, although in fragments. On the radio, Nyipir and Ajany hear that people are being chased from their homes and those who stay are chopped up and burnt, and that Kofi Annan has come to resolve the impasse (Owuor 2014, 67). Kibaki and Raila, the main contenders of the presidential elections, finally signed a peace agreement after two months of violence (69).

> The Trader sighs. '*Aieee*! Godless news.' [...] A fisherman left his home on the day after the [vote] counting. He went to Lake Navaisha. [...] He left his wives — there were two, and eight children in their house. But when he was on the water, neighbours wrote out his name and those of his wives and children. Neighbours whom he brought fish. They wrote out his name and gave it to demons that came to seal his house, pour petrol, strike a match, and dance while the family inside died screaming. Those neighbours watched. They ate food. (83)

As Kenya was trying to come to terms with the violence, Petrus Keah and Ali Dida Hada converse and ponder a peace rally from Dandora to Kangemi while they wonder whether a local tribunal will help the country heal. Petrus asks, 'But, as people, do we even want to live together?' (257). The violence demystified the notion that Kenya was an island of peace and tranquillity (Somerville 2009, 528) as Kenyans had lived under the illusion that Kenya *hakuna matata.* Ogot (2010) observes that since independence, Kenyans had lived believing that they are one nation but ' ... when the lid was suddenly raised, and the explosion occurred, they discovered that they are a deeply and perilous fractured society ... the forces of intolerance, of hate and exclusion were on the rise ... ' (191).

Regarding the 2007–2008 post-election violence, Matthew Carotenuto and Brett Shadle (2012) argue that as the violence took place, the world media reverted to tales of mindless 'tribal' violence perpetrated by machete-wielding young men. They point out that what the popular narrative often failed to capture was the continuity with Kenya's violent colonial past. Their thought is that the roots of violence are traced to as far back as the colonial era when public violence was employed to assert social and political authority (1–2). Although they argue that the roots of violence stemmed from the colonial period, there are also deep-seated issues such as ethnicity and unfair distribution of resources since independence.

According to Nic Cheeseman (2008), salient ethno-regional identities reinforced by historical grievances over land ownership, economic inequality and political exclusion are central to an understanding of the Kenya crisis. Cheeseman adds that the spread of the violence in Kenya owed much to the informalisation of the state, the diffusion of violence beyond central control, and the rise of militias connected to the political elite (167). After the signing of the peace agreement, Kenyans embarked on the usual crusade messages calling upon Kenyans to forgive and forget, and forge a more united Kenya. This scenario points to the national myths of unity created during independence for Kenyans to unite despite their ethnic differences. After Kibaki and Raila signed a peace agreement, the coalition government launched *Operation Rudi Nyumbani* to resettle Kenyans who had been displaced by the violence. The government was in haste to resettle the displaced people without first spearheading an honest reconciliation process.

Conclusion

Based on intersection of history and fiction in *Dust,* Owuor fictionalises history to depict suppressed colonial and postcolonial stories. Through stories of fictitious characters such as Nyipir, Akai, Ajany, Ali, Odidi, Hugh Bolton and Petrus Keah intertwined with historical events, Owuor attempts to explore why violence, torture, assassinations, disillusionment and corruption are silent in Kenya's official history and have persisted in Kenya from the colonial to the postcolonial period. The novel also attempts to explain why we seem to have normalised and accepted the ills as a nation. It emerges from the analysis above that official history has assembled historical events that portray the nation-state positively while ignoring and de-emphasising stories on the margin, especially when they paint a bad picture of the nation-state. *Dust,* therefore, voices such suppressed narratives to expose the gaps in official history.

Note

1. This paper is an abridged Chapter of my MA Literature Thesis *Narrating Kenyan History through Fiction in Yvonne Owuor's Dust* presented for the award of the degree of Master of Arts in Literature, University of Nairobi, August 2015.

Disclosure Statement

No potential conflict of interest was reported by the author.

References

Agho, Jude. 1993. "Disillusionment and Alienation in the Novels of Ngugi wa Thiong'o, Ayi Kwei Armah, Alex La Guma and Sembene Ousmane." Unpublished PhD Thesis, University of Ibadan.

Anderson, Benedict. 1983. *Imagined Communities: Reflections on the Origin and Spread of Nationalism*. London: Verso.

Blumenson, Martin. 1963. "Can Official History be Honest History?" Web *Military Affairs* 26 (4): 153–61. doi:10.2307/1985610.

Carotenut, Matthew, and Brett Shadle. 2012. "Introduction: Toward a History of Violence in Colonial Kenya." Web *International Journal of African Historical Studies* 4S (1): 1–7.

Cheeseman, Nic. 2008. "The Kenyan Elections of 2007: An Introduction." Web *Journal of Eastern African Studies* 2 (2): 166–184. doi:10.1080/17531050802058286.

Hobsbawm, John Ernest, ed. 1990. *Nations and Nationalism Since 1780: Programme, Myth, Reality*. Cambridge: Cambridge University Press.

Hornsby, Charles. 2012. *Kenya: A History Since Independence*. London: I.B. Tauris. doi:10.5040/9780755619023.

Kantai, Parselelo. 2009. "Tom Mboya: The Untold Story." *Daily Nation*, July 3. https://allafrica.com/stories/200907061153.html.

Lucheli, Isaiah. 2013. "Pattni Walks to Freedom as Charges Dropped". *Standard on Saturday*, May 4.

Narayan, Badri. 2007. "Imagining the Past and Reconstructing Histories." Web *Social Scientist* 35 (9/10): 67–87.

Ogot, Bethwell. 2010. *Who, If Any One, Owns the Past? Reflections on the Meaning of 'Public History.'* Kisumu: Anyange Press.

Oja, F. Matt. 1988. "Fictional History and Historical Fiction: Solzhenitsyn and Kiš as Exemplars." Web *History and Theory* 27 (2): 111–124. doi:10.2307/2505136.

Opondo, P. A. 2014. "Ethnic politics and post-election violence of 2007/8 in Kenya African." Web *Journal of History and Culture*. 6 (4): 59–67.

Osoba, S. O. 1996. "Corruption in Nigeria: Historical Perspectives." *Review of African Political Economy* 69 (69): 371–86. doi:10.1080/03056249608704203.

Owuor, Yvonne. 2014. *Dust*. London: Knopf.

Simatei, Tirop. 2005. "Colonial Violence, Postcolonial Violations: Violence, Landscape, and Memory in Kenyan Fiction." Web *Research in African Literatures* 36 (2): 85–94. doi:10.2979/RAL.2005.36.2.85.

Somerville, Keith. 2009. "British Media Coverage of the Post-election Violence in Kenya, 2007–08." *Journal of Eastern African Studies* 3 (3): 526–542. doi:10.1080/17531050903273776.

Taylor, Alastair MacDonald. 1938. "The Historical Novel: As a Source in History." *The Sewanee Review* 46 (4): 459–479. Web.

Truth, Justice and Reconciliation Commission. 2013. *Report of the Truth, Justice and Reconciliation Commission*. Nairobi: TJRC.

White, Hayden. 1987. *The Content of the Form: Narrative Discourse and Historical Representation*. Baltimore, Md.: Johns Hopkins UP.

White, Hayden. 2005. "Rethinking History." Web *International Journal of African Historical Studies* 9 (2/3): 147–157.

Let's Talk About Craft! A Conversation with Yvonne Adhiambo Owuor

Tina Steiner

Kenya-born Yvonne Adhiambo Owuor studied English and History at Kenyatta University, earned a Master of Arts at the University of Reading in the UK, and an MPhil from the University of Queensland, Australia. Her short story, "The Weight of Whispers" earned her the Caine Prize for African Writing in 2003. The narrative takes the perspective of an aristocratic refugee who escapes genocide in his unnamed country to go into exile in Kenya with his family. Her highly acclaimed debut novel, *Dust* (2014) explores the state of the nation through the lives of a dysfunctional multi-ethnic family centred in the north of Kenya. A tragic loss forces the bereaved family to work through their secrets and silences. Owuor's second novel, *The Dragonfly Sea*, published in 2019 is a coming-of-age story of a precocious little girl named Ayaana, who lives with her mother on Pate, an island off the coast of Kenya, bombarded by the forces of history, time, nature and geopolitics.

Owuor's short stories and essays have been published in a few international journals and magazines, including the *New Daughters of Africa* anthology. One of these, "The Knife Grinder's Tale" was adapted as a short film in 2007. Owuor has been honoured by her country for her artistic and cultural contributions, including a Head of State Commendation in 2018. In 2005 she was invited to participate in the International Writing Program at the University of Iowa, and again in 2017, when she returned as the first IWP Grinnell Fellow. In 2010, as a participant in the Pilgrimages project initiated by the Chinua Achebe Center, she travelled to Kinshasa and recounted her experiences in a travelogue titled "Milobela". In 2017 she was the artist-in-residence at the Stellenbosch Institute for Advanced Study. In 2018/19 Owuor was a Fellow at the Wissenschaftskolleg zu Berlin, and, later, at the Institute d'études avancées de Nantes. She was the 2020 Dorothea Schlegel Artist-in-Residence, attached to the Freie Universität Berlin, EXC 2020 Temporal Communities project. Owuor previously worked as the Executive Director of the Zanzibar International Film Festival/Festival of the Dhow Countries (2003-5), a computer technologist, and an arts academic programme curriculum developer. She is involved with creative content development initiatives, (bespoke) arts event production, and Africa-Asia trans-oceanic conversations. The author currently operates out of Nairobi.

TS: How and when did you know that you are a writer? Would you consider it a calling and what does that mean to you?

YAO: At different phases:

a) As a precocious toddler discovering that letters created words that turned into images within that could be 'regurgitated' by means of chalk and my parents' walls.
b) In primary school, the shiest of shy students using words to write my first poem, a Christmas one, and the teacher, Mrs Saunders called my mother in to confirm that I did not copy it from a book.
c) The composition and language As, the other subjects Cs and Ds.
d) When the very first short story I wrote as an adult went public and won me an award ("Weight of Whispers", Caine Prize 2003).
e) Years later, fleeing what I had become professionally, 'letting go' is the correct phrase, and choosing writing. It is in Australia doing the MPhil for Creative Writing, the Me, Me, Me degree, doing the degree my heart had long wanted rather than a study that was 'right, proper, explainable to others', that was when I slipped into the jersey 'Writer' without a twitch or twinge.

Writing a calling? In some cases. Mine too, I guess. When the muses finally wrestled me to the ground and detached me from my corporate inclinations, there was the sense of coming to a place of familiarity at last, of a peace that persisted despite no sense or idea of how or where or if I would earn a living from giving myself over to the literary and story life. What this means to me is something very simple: I can answer with equanimity the question that once pierced and shattered my complacency: What would you regret not doing the most if you were to die now? My answer now (not then): I did it.

TS: What are the most rewarding and replenishing aspects of writing for you, what the most fearfully difficult? How do you overcome or work with the challenges?

YAO: A sense of homecoming, of giving self over to the art, the pleasure of applying words on a previously blank page/screen, the sense of world-building as the story grows, the often-painful quest — although this takes so much out, it does put more back in. Challenges: there to be figured out. Like story. Making sense of things. I love slipping into story world and looking around, retrieving unexpected characters and story-scapes. I love the 'laboratory' of books to read from all over the world; I am a book hoarder, unfortunately. So I have a room of unread books that greet me like unchosen partners in a *milonga*. Yet I need them around me, read or unread: writing and reading go hand in glove. Overcoming challenges? Different ones appear at different phases of the writing journey: dealt with, in my case, inelegantly. My fundamental one is that of acquiring a martial discipline to do the work of writing. The story might exist in full in my imagination. The act of actually writing it, entering into the 'dojo' of the creative space is such a struggle for me. But once I am in, that's cool. It is getting out that becomes the battle.

TS: How do you nurture your ideas for possible projects and where do they come from? I am wondering here about the relationship between the interior life of the imagination and dreams and exterior impulses like historical events and geographical realities. Are there patterns you can identify?

YAO: Senses in the world; everyday encounters, feelings, watching the human being, witnessing to life, witness of life unfolding; the big themes that never grow old, like death, meaning, belonging, what it means to be human here and now; what the humanity of the other means, here and now, where here and now also means life as a continuum. I don't identify patterns, I merely enter spaces where there are no demarcation lines or boundaries between inner and outer worlds, including dream worlds.

TS: In your work you have compared writing to map-making. I am intrigued by that analogy. Do you see yourself as a cartographer? What kind of worlds are you mapping in your work and what maps are you writing against?

YAO: In the innermost part of my being, I do imagine myself as a cartographer of worlds with, through words, working with words to write a world, more particularly myriad African worlds and their dimensionality. I am a walker, a hiker, a traveller who relishes entering into spaces far from home. But I do not navigate these using conventional maps. I can neither tell my left from my right without having to mimic writing (right is the hand I write with). But if I have read of the place in fiction or non-fiction, or experienced it in a film or a song, I sense my way through it moved by the feelings the story inspired. My cartography fascination comes from not knowing how. Yet I am enthralled by what word-maps/stories reveal in the strange geographies they summon, in the paths, and signposts they propose. I sometimes buy atlases to look through and imagine myself here, there and elsewhere. It is a habit I picked up in childhood. We used to do that with my sisters. Today, I guess, I 'map' in-between worlds with words, the ones that have fallen through contemporary history's crevices, and mostly, but not restricted, to African worlds. Yes, perhaps a storyteller can also be called a word-cartographer of human interstices.

TS: What have you learned in your writing life that you wish you had known when you started out? What advice would you give to aspiring writers who are at the beginning of their journey?

YAO: I wish I had learned much sooner that a calling, a vocation can also be artistic and pleasurable. Because I loved books so much, right from childhood, it took such a long time to realise that entering their world could also be the basis of my future, the means through which I could engage and navigate the world. Later, overwhelmed by the size of the road, I wish I had known that fear is an over-rated force, that the story-teller's first act should be an act of murder: kill the critic, including and especially the inner critic; that to be fragile and uncertain before a blank page is normal, necessary and is part of the creative journey — it is not a flaw or failure. The right demeanor is to receive the creative and imaginative 'energies' in gratitude, peace and expectation. To the aspiring, beginning writer, the right time to start writing is now. Also, the acquisition and training in craft never, ever, ever ends. And finally, read. Read ecumenically, widely, wildly and madly. And the unknown is your companion, teacher and friend. I hear that many are told to 'write what you know'; I maintain, write what you are most curious about, what you likely do not know, that which will drive you to question, seek, discover and find fresh lexica for.

ORCID iD

Tina Steiner http://orcid.org/0000-0002-3083-778X

References

Owuor, Yvonne Adhiambo. 2003. "The Weight of Whispers". *Kwani? Journal*. Ed. Binyavanga Wainaina. Nairobi: Kwani Trust.

Owuor, Yvonne Adhiambo. 2014. *Dust*. Nairobi: Kwani Trust.

Owuor, Yvonne Adhiambo. 2019. *The Dragonfly Sea*. New York: Knopf.

Index

For Product Safety Concerns and Information please contact our EU representative GPSR@taylorandfrancis.com
Taylor & Francis Verlag GmbH, Kaufingerstraße 24, 80331 München, Germany

www.ingramcontent.com/pod-product-compliance
Lightning Source LLC
Chambersburg PA
CBHW081358090726
47908CB00011B/2716
* 9 7 8 1 0 3 2 4 0 8 2 6 2 *